CONTAMINATION

Written by

Dave Jeffery

Based on a Story by

Jason Wright

Dead Silent Publishing

deadsilentpublishing.co.uk

CONTAMINATION

Story Copyright © Jason Wright

Text Copyright © Dave Jeffery

Cover artwork by Danielle Tunstall

Book design by Donnie Light

Edited by Patti Geesey

TODAY

The screams come from far away. The glass screen helps to muffle them, but on days when the lab isn't busy they come as a thin, woeful drone, relentless and pitiful.

People move behind the glass; they all wear white coats and surgical masks. They mill around tables made from stainless steel, tables which are currently empty. They aren't always. Most times the things that make the distant screams lie upon them. They are scary to look at, but there is knowledge that the creatures are part of helping to save lives.

Someone steps up to the glass. The world is filled with the image of a man. He has a stern face softened by the lines beneath eyes of watery grey. He smiles and all of the omnipotent fear melts away.

'How are you feeling?'

'Better,' Dean says. 'The pain is gone. When can I come out?'

'In time,' the man says. 'We need to make sure you're no longer sick. Make sure you don't hurt other people.'

'How long? It's scary in here.'

'I know.' The man nods to reinforce the statement. 'But you want to be well, don't you? You want to help other people get well?'

'Yes, but I'm lonely,' Dean says. Inside, a terrible longing for the company of others threatens to swamp him. He can feel tears running down his cheeks.

'There, there,' the man says. The grey eyes appear to be moist in sympathy. 'Shall I sing to you?'

'Yes,' Dean says. 'I'd like that.'

'Go to your bed and I shall sing your favourite song until you go to sleep.'

Dean moves away from the glass, but he is reluctant. Every emotion is telling him to stay near to the man behind the glass. He goes to the small bed and lies down, taking the heavy duvet and dragging it over him.

Through the intercom the man in the lab coat sings. The words are soothing and sleep rises up to claim him. As he is sucked into oblivion, the song goes with him, keeping him company like a good friend through a great ordeal.

* * *

'Ah, shit!'

Dean Sharp's alarm clock was set to eleven thirty am. While this was usual, no matter what day of the week or what time of year, the buzz-saw din of an alarm going off was not the reason he sat bolt upright in his bed.

Confused and disorientated, he tried to focus on the room about him. Despite the dim bulb overhead, the light still played with his eyes and sent needles into his brain.

Somewhere in these moments he heard the dull thud of a bottle of Jim Beam hitting the carpet. He made no move to investigate. The bottle would be empty.

It always was.

He glanced over at the clock, and it told him bad news.

Eight forty am.

'Fuck me,' he muttered as he rubbed his hands through his dark, unruly hair. He couldn't remember the last time he'd done an eight-forty. Maybe twenty years ago at Sheffield University when he'd studied for his BA in journalism. Back then it was all about early doors at the Victoria Inn and another day of assignment rewrites with a pie and a pint as *Ultravox* played on the jukebox.

The memories were good and he was reluctant to let them go. He could almost hear the clink of beer glasses. No, not the clink of beer glasses, but glass, yes.

Breaking glass.

As the sheets slid from his bed it wasn't only the cool breeze that came to him through the window of his Islington flat. Both elements sent a shiver through his body, goosing his skin in the process.

Buffered by the curtains, thin distant screams rose from the streets below. He scuttled out of bed, his boxer shorts askew and exposing him to a picture of a semi-clad Anna Torv on the wall before he absently adjusted them.

Not now, baby, he thought. *Later you'll get my undivided.*

He walked at pace towards the window and inched the curtain aside. He peered out onto the scene three storeys below. No matter how many times he blinked his hazel eyes, the images outside remained the same.

Crowds of people below were fighting. No, not fighting, brawling; on the pavements and in the gutters. Men and women scrabbling around on the ground, on each other, some being beaten with bare hands and feet; vicious nails- be they finely manicured or unkempt talons- tearing at faces, trying to find soft flesh in unprotected sockets. There were children too, without rhyme or reason, brandishing everyday objects: a cricket bat, a hammer, a chisel, but their conventional use was obsolete in this *New World Disorder*. Now, hammers were brought down on skulls, cricket bats were used to pummel backs of legs and flailing hands, and chisels were rammed into soft bellies until the grey streets ran red.

From his vantage point, Dean was an omnipotent, impotent god looking down upon a world that had gone insane. He stumbled away from the window and vomited onto the floor, his legs giving out and his hands planted in sick to prevent him from collapsing onto the carpet. He threw up again, more this time, onto his hands and upper arms. The vomit was hot and shocking against his skin. His sides ached from the force of it. Another retch, but it fetched only bile that he spat out regardless.

'What the fuck's going on? Did I miss the memo?'

Rhetoric: all of it, spilling out through the snot and tears. He came up onto his knees, crossing his arms, oblivious to the vomit now slopping against his chest and dripping into his lap.

Check the news, idiot!

The thought punched through his head like a falling...

Hammer

...meteor and had him moving to the door that separated his bedroom from the rest of the apartment.

He made for the lounge where his forty-two inch plasma waited, and its screen was dark as though a portent for the images to come. He stopped briefly at the kitchen, a place of pale wood and sombre, storm-cloud grey granite, and grabbed a tea towel which he used to mop up the mess congealing on his arms as he staggered up the short hallway to the lounge.

There, black leather sofas and bright yellow walls waited for him. Opposite, an expanse of glass showed the city skyline, framed by a PVC fascia. He slowly walked towards the panes and stared, his mouth forming an 'O' without him even being aware of it.

Beyond the glass, beyond belief, the city was burning.

* * *

Smoke belched into the sky, cavorting and swirling; black bellowing bellies painted yellow by the multiple infernos that created them.

Dean planted his hands on the panes in order to steady himself. His mind echoed the sky; a swirling maelstrom of dark, brooding clouds, not fuelled by destruction but by the confusion that came with processing the images beyond the window. His breath jittered as it emerged from his mouth.

'This can't be happening,' he said. In his head it sounded lame, out in the ether it became an embarrassing conclusion born from self-delusion. This shit was happening. He just needed to know how bad it was and how widespread it had become.

I will be with you. Be patient, my love.

Another abstract thought. He was prone to them, especially in times of stress. And he was out-of-his-skull stressed at that moment. He wished it didn't happen; it only topped up the pressure. He had Jenna to thank for it.

Not now, Deano. Not when you really need to keep your shit wired tight. Another time, another place; just not fucking now.

He forced himself to move away from the window; the ghostly images of his hands waved him on his way before fading as though abandoning him to his fate. He picked up the TV remote, the black plastic squeaking under his taut grip as he hit the buttons. Dean jumped as a huge blast of static filled the lounge. His legs caught the edge of the rosewood coffee table and he fell heavily onto one of the sofas where the leather squealed like an old man's wet fart.

Dean aimed the remote at the TV and punched the keys as he fervently rubbed at his shin. A horizontal red weal rose to the surface of his pale skin as, on the screen, words made the pain fade to nothing for the time he read them and realised their connotations.

Do not panic. Wait for instructions.

Six words, two basic sentences, on every channel, white letters on a ditch-dark background. They screamed an epiphany in his beleaguered brain as his throat yearned for a shot of Jim Beam. Six words telling him how things were from this point on.

Dean got conservative; he summed things up in four.

'We are so fucked,' he croaked.

* * *

He had an eighty-year-old father in Birmingham and a spinster sister in Sussex. He'd seen neither in more than fifteen years. The argument had been heated and laced with venom, festering emotions stockpiled from a misplaced childhood, but time had rendered the altercation meaningless; the relationships no longer just dysfunctional, estrangement had set up stall, too. The passing years blunted the edges enough for occasional stilted telephone conversations and the ritualistic posting of Christmas and birthday cards.

Logistics provided enough cover from which to hide the apathy of a family that had become cemented in place by duty. The mortar was aged and crumbling but, at that moment, as Dean climbed from the shower and towelled himself off, his need to see his kin was overwhelming.

Shit, it takes the end of the world to make me want to see Jenna.
End of the World?

He paused. Had he fallen asleep and missed a few stops? He tried to drag the events of the previous night through a mind made fudge by booze and fear. He thought he'd gone to his usual haunt, a bar deep in the suburbs, where whisky was served by the bottle and people left you alone.

Shadows of the past came to him. He recalled stumbling through streets jaundiced by lamplight; witnessing a couple kissing in a bus shelter, and the bark of a vixen in a distant alleyway.

Grey and slurry slow, but these memories were returning and all of them made plain something he already knew. Last night, after he'd got home and downed his second bottle of Old Jim, he'd passed out. But the world he'd winked out of for a while was normal. No burning buildings, no orgy of violence where children cracked skulls with claw hammers, no streets made wet with the blood of the slaughtered.

Oh, come on, Deano! Face it. You wouldn't know last night from last week when you're on a bender.

Yeah. But shit-faced or not, I'd know if people were killing each other. When I went to bed, the world wasn't like this.

You're a piss-head. Don't talk in absolutes.

They were his thoughts but in his head he saw Jenna, heard her voice. His sister was thirty-six and successful. She had business acumen, which translated to Dean as being a total, Cavalli-clad bitch. And then some. With a cherry on it.

The arguments had been bad when they were growing up, Jenna always the centre of the family universe. This tenet became even more prevalent after their mother had died. Hit and run, the police had said. It mattered not, his mum was dead and his life was a huge shit burger he choked on for most of his youth. And Jenna was the short order cook who was always happy to keep that particular meal on the menu with her constant digs, constant bleating. Always wanting, needing, things her way. His father was a good, yet hardened, soul. But Sharp Senior had been made soft by the death of his wife, and he saw too much of his dearly departed in Jenna. The emotional transference was perhaps inevitable, but when it happened it wasn't so much applied as slapped on good and thick. The upshot was that Dean's sister could do, say and have what she wanted as long as she pandered to her father's emotional needs, and left her brother to count down the days when he could get the hell out of the house for good.

The mini wars of childhood had given way to bitter battles, tempered by a parting of ways when Dean left home to attend university, effectively cutting himself off from the life he once knew and loathed. He would've loved to have said that he'd never looked back, but such a claim would have a suffix of 'pants on fire' had he ever made it. He did look back, especially when too much whisky craned his neck. In the past he saw answers as to why his life sucked.

But that was before he'd seen the city in flames. Life sucks but this new reality didn't just bite, it stayed around to chow down for a while, and citizens were mere meat, tenderised by its powerful jaws.

How many people are dead? How can I find out just how bad things really are?

TV was as good as useless. Dean's mind went through a check list as he dragged on a white shirt and jeans. He hunted through the apartment for his mobile phone and found it in the white-tiled bathroom, abandoned, by the sink unit.

He yanked the cell from the basin, knocking over the ceramic mug that housed his toothbrush, paste and razor. The items clattered onto the floor; the mug toppled like a drunk on the edge of a kerb then it fell onto the tiles where it exploded like a small, noisy bomb.

But this was a distant event. Dean was too focused on the mobile rammed to his ear. He checked the display countless times and it made clear he had a full battery and the signal was good.

But the earpiece gave out only static.

Dean shook the device, his frustration surfacing as a fierce beast. He managed to wrestle with it, dragging its carcass beneath the waves. It had no place here, not yet at least. But he knew it wasn't far away, instead, it lurked on the ocean floor waiting for the riptide to drag him down where it could rise up and consume him.

Now what? Sit tight and wait it out?

He turned to the basics, scanned the kitchen and checked out whether he had the provisions to see him through a few days. The food was rudimentary, the cuisine of a bachelor pad. In a wall-mounted cupboard he found tins of processed food he'd never knew existed, let alone touched.

For a moment, the thought of food turned his stomach. This was nothing new when he'd spent a couple of days in the company of Ol' Jim. But this felt deeper than that, this felt fundamental; innate like some kind of primordial warning. Then, like a passing thought, it was gone, and he continued to scan his provisions.

Maybe the tins weren't even his. More likely they were the leftovers of another relationship that had gone south. At least this time he had something to show for it, even though it was almost as unpalatable as the loneliness.

He continued his search. A check of the cupboards, fridge and freezer established he'd enough assorted foodstuff to last a week.

Thank God for microwaves.

As long as the power stays on, Deano.

He ignored Jenna's troublesome voice in his head.

'Sniff my shit, bitch!' he whispered.

But Jenna's voice was insistent, like an angry wasp trapped in an upended glass.

You got enough Jim Beam on tap, Deano? You got enough to keep those shakes at bay? You can do without food, but what about a few days without Ol' Jim?

Panic, then a surging tsunami almost making the room do a three sixty. He gripped the breakfast bar in order to stay on his feet. The source of the fear was a sudden, shocking realisation that one thing was missing.

No booze. Not one fucking drop.

Despite what he already knew, he went through the motions. He rechecked cupboards, opened drawers, and yanked the heavy stainless steel door of the American freezer. Desperation was the food in his belly; his heart pounded like a starving hand on a baker's window.

In the lounge, scatter cushions lived up to their job description as Dean hurled them across the room. Seat covers were upended and the coffee table knocked askew in his frenzied search.

The bedroom now, with its vomit-splattered carpet putting an acrid reek in his nostrils. The mattress was dragged from the bed frame, the wardrobe doors thrown wide and strewn clothes created a mountain in the middle of the floor, where the sick tide lapped against the fabric shoreline.

Through it all, Dean sobbed; eyes blurred and his emotions supercharged. Not an hour before, he had looked upon a scene where, like the reaper in Brunel's *Triumph of Death* painting, he had watched humanity literally tear itself apart on the streets below. All of this was forgotten, his misery had jumped on board and there was mutiny below decks.

For the second time that morning, Anna Torv watched Dean Sharp crumple to his knees. He balled his hands into fists and rammed them against his mouth to mask the scream of rage ripping through his throat.

There was no sitting tight. Not for now at least. He had to go beyond the walls of his flat.

Before the absence of Ol' Jim had him climbing them.

* * *

'You've got to be out of your mind, Dean,' he said to his reflection in the lounge window as he considered leaving his pseudo-sanctuary.

To his left, a small squat building - home on alternate days to the indoor market -saw its doors ripped open by a dull blast that scattered debris out into the streets. There were pieces of people in the wreckage. Red wads of flesh lay amongst the sugar sparkle glass and splintered wood. 'Out of your fucking mind.'

Not quite madness, though. That would be coming later when the last residue of Ol' Jim was processed and pissed into the pan, and his influence would be popping out for a while. And, without another appointment pending, Dean's body would mourn Ol' Jim's passing in ways that brought tremors, aching bones and the bright memories of a childhood best left behind. Drink as a means of survival was his father's gift to him. Not one that could be wrapped in shiny paper and stowed under the tree, of course, but certainly one Dean had held in safekeeping for as long as he could remember.

Be strong, my love. You will never be alone. I will always be with you.

He blinked the thought away. He had one too many of them bouncing around his skull already. The ones with no meaning whatsoever were officially surplus to requirement at the best of times. Today they really needed to *fuck right off.*

'I need it,' he said to the burning city. 'I need it to survive.'

He pawed at his face and sucked in air. Against the skin of his cheeks, he could feel the shudder in his hands as his body began its lament. He'd no choice. But the decision for this had been made years ago, when he'd chosen to open his mouth on the neck of a bottle rather than his eyes to the world of contrition.

In the here and now, no amount of self-abasement was going to change a thing. He had to go in search of booze.

And he had to go *now.*

* * *

Dean peered through the spy hole in the front door to his apartment. The tiny portal was smudged by something; a dirty brown substance smeared upon the lens. He couldn't see a thing.

'Fuck it.'

He turned his head and placed an ear to the smooth surface. The wood was cold on his pinna; the bread knife hard in his hand.

He held his breath and listened.

Silence.

This should have been a good thing but it merely added to Dean's pervading sense of dysfunction. This was a busy building in a bustling suburb. There should have been something coming from behind the door; even now he expected to hear a TV's static hiss, or the thumps of people moving around.

Maybe people gouging each other's eyes out?

He would take it as it was. He wouldn't need to go far. There were several other apartments on his floor. Any one of them would have booze. It was the twenty-first century's most common painkiller, after all.

Dean brought the knife up and fumbled with the door chain. He slid the lock into its track. The brass links rattled under the combined influence of fear and withdrawal.

Once the chain was in place, Dean unlocked the door; the internal deadbolts were loud as they disengaged from their tumblers and caused him to wince. He waited for a few seconds, despite his body's need urging him to open the goddamned door and give it the only medicine its disease understood.

He slowly pulled the door open, the only sound coming from the chain as it paid out the slack. He placed his face into the widening crack, and the warm air wafting from the corridor beyond brought with it a ghastly stink that had him retching within seconds.

The stench was sweet and purulent, and he knew it instantly. He knew it because last summer he'd left a steak out on the breakfast bar and, instead of returning home to eat it, had gone out on a two-day bender. By the time he returned, the central heating had done its thing and microbiology pulled up to the party. The flat had carried the same sickly stink for three days afterwards.

And here it was again, rotting meat assailing his nostrils and turning his stomach to water. In sympathy with his churning guts, his eyes spilled tears.

Dean took a huge breath and clamped his hand over his nose and mouth. He peeped into the corridor, his vision misted until he blinked it clear.

The corridor was in darkness save for a rectangular slab of light falling out onto the carpeted floor. In the light, Dean could make out an uneven shape lying inert with a mist of flies hovering about it. Their sound came to him, a vile buzzing that recalled only images of filth and corruption.

A body. There's a fucking body on my landing.

This shit is too close to home, Deano, Jenna warned. *You sure you want to go looking for Ol' Jim and bring him home? Maybe you should just go get the Audi TT and get the fucker into sixth as fast as you can.*

He shut out the thoughts. Despite the body, other more pressing realisations were dawning on him. The slab of light meant a door to another apartment was open. The unattended body meant that the apartment was empty and, therefore, safe.

He knew the people in the apartment only as Mr and Mrs Marshall. He didn't know them, didn't link arms and sing Auld Lang Syne on New Year's Eve. They were merely neighbours he wished a good morning from time to time. Now one of them was lying in the hall, still and stinking.

Focus, Deano! You need to go and check out the apartment. You need to go and disturb those flies from their blown banquet and seek out some Ol' Jim or a close cousin. Do it or you may as well lie down and let the bluebottles fuck you good and hard, and become an incubator for their wriggling, squirming offspring.

Dean nodded an accord, his private reflections saying just enough, giving him grounds to continue. He closed the door and returned to the kitchen, where a damp tea towel was dowsed with soapy detergent. He placed the scented cloth over his nose and mouth. Within moments, he had opened the door and stepped out into a dark and uncertain world.

* * *

The light from his apartment gave Dean some comfort. He'd left the door at forty-five degrees and was using it as a beacon in the gloom. His destination was only thirty yards away and, as he neared, he could see the flies as a black, undulating fog.

The luminescence from his own apartment was now waning, and he found himself in a twilight netherworld of his home and the source of this perilous quest.

He moved with suppressed urgency and caution, caught between the craving for booze and the need to be safe, yet all the time having difficulty separating one from the other. His foot caught something solid and he almost went down. He staggered and reached out to steady himself on the nearest wall. His hand found something firm and it supported him for a moment before yielding with a soft crack. His hand became wet with a substance that was both thick and so pungent it threatened to neutralise his temporary mask.

You know what that stuff is, Deano, Jenna was muttering again. *It's body juice. Dead man's fat running through your fingers. Are you really that desperate to see Ol' Jim again? Can't you smell the corruption on you? In you? Cough it up, dear brother. You're a goddamned mess.*

'Can't you leave me be?' he snarled and rushed for the other apartment, head down, his soiled hand outstretched and silhouetted against the oncoming light. As he ran, his splayed fingers appeared corrugated by the glove of dead meat about them. Wads of goo fell away like a leper's diseased flesh.

He was soon at the body caught in the light from the apartment. Perhaps 'body' was too conservative; it implied something that had substance and human form. Dean's reaction was to slow down as he approached the mangled, mutilated figure lying in front of the door.

Not a body, Jenna said. *Fucking remains, Deano.*

It was difficult to distinguish clothes from flesh; everything was tattered and ruined. The remnants of a head stared up at the ceiling, eyes gone and mouth wide in a silent eternal scream from lips bloated by trauma. Dean couldn't make out if it was Mr or Mrs Marshall, but he realised quickly that the skull may have been aimed at the ceiling but the body was lying face down. Any remaining flesh was flyblown and the corpse's offspring wavered close by, the way a filthy cloud hangs over a foundry.

The rules have changed, Deano. Jenna again.

Why didn't the bitch just fuck off?

But she wasn't fucking off, was she? No, she was there as she'd always been in the earlier days of his life.

Can't you see you have to get out, get free? It's only a matter of time before you end up in a chum bucket. That what you want? Is that what you're prepared to sacrifice for another swing of Ol' Jim?

The rhetoric drove him on. He went right, his hand out to part the curtain of flies hanging in the air. They bounced against his forehead as he stepped into the apartment. Some of them were reluctant to leave him, their primitive senses excited by the scum on his hand. He could see the congealed red and grey goo in detail. The viscous fluid was interspersed with flecks of bone, and hair turned dark with blood.

The layout inside was different to that of his own apartment and Dean's search for any room where he could rid himself of the vile, stinking mass on his hand was frenetic, irrespective of the potential unseen dangers. His was base need, the desire to be rid of a terrible burden overriding anything else.

He found the kitchen after opening two doors that revealed only bedrooms, both of which were neat and sparse, each with a single bed draped in blanched linen. At the head of each bed, on stark magnolia walls, was a small cross and a picture of the Virgin Mary.

The kitchen was less restrained and gave an idea as to the pervading panic in the final moments of a life. A pan stained with red, congealed sauce sat on the ceramic hob, a wooden spoon sticking out of it like an antennae trying to pull a signal out of the putrid ether. The work surfaces were cluttered and, on a central isle where pots and pans hung from the ceiling on an iron frame, an upended drawer sat like a statement to the chaos afflicting the world. The drawer had been pulled from a nearby cupboard with such force its metal runners were twisted and its carcass listed to one side, prevented from toppling by the pan tree overhead, and spilling its silver guts all over the worktop.

Panic happened in here, Deano, Jenna said in his head. *A frenzy, like the world turned in an instant for the Marshalls. One minute it's soup for supper. The next, it's mauled remains in the doorway.*

He went for the sink unit and allowed the towel to come away from his mouth as he turned the faucet. The sound of the water hitting the stainless steel basin was loud and startling. Dean held his breath and ducked. He pulled open a cupboard and rooted around for detergent. He found washing-up liquid and coated his goo-covered hand with slime of a fragrant sort.

He let the stale air go from his lungs and breathed through his mouth for a while. It was a trick he'd learned early in his career. Rooting through bins for pieces of information to support a story wasn't a practice he was proud of these days. Back then he was just starting out, naïve and hungry for the scoop that would win him a Pulitzer.

The water from the faucet remained cold, but Dean cleaned off the vile substance from his hand. He risked a quick sniff of the air and relished the sharp pine scent the washing-up liquid gave off.

His hands still wet, Dean turned to the real task. He'd not seen any evidence of booze so far but he remained hopeful. He started on the cupboards in the kitchen, his heart buoyant with the idea of finding liquid comfort, the kind that warmed the throat and numbed the brain. He exhausted the cupboards without success. Part of the enthusiasm -

the certainty that he'd find something - took a hit. He brushed it off, but the bruise on his confidence remained.

Dean made for the lounge where two Chesterfield armchairs each kept company by an occasional table. Two beds and two tables; all the signs of a relationship that was out of gas but still managing to run on empty.

Dean knew the portents well. He'd seen them once too often in the news stories he'd covered when working for the local press in Birmingham: sad stories that ended with a guy getting up and slaughtering his partner then feeding himself both barrels of a twelve bore or maybe going extreme trainspotting on a railway line.

The writing desk by the veranda window was an old thing made of dark wood and festooned with silver picture frames. Behind it, through the lace curtains, Dean could see a different part of the city but the columns of smoke were the same. As he got to the desk his eyes flitted to the frames. A past was edged in silver; a man and a woman holding hands in a black and white, faded photograph. The frame held an inscription: 'Harold and Maud. Brighton, 1955'. The same couple was in the picture next to it, older and with a child in a pushchair. They all had smiles, but Harold Marshall seemed to have a distant look in his eyes, as though wishing for another life. More frames told how a family grew up: a daughter in a park, then at a prom and finally a graduation shot. Mum and Dad and a beautiful blonde woman in an academic gown and mitre; a family growing up without hint of how they had come to grow apart. Just the man's eyes in every picture: distant and rueful.

Dean fumbled in the desk, seeking out drawers and moving papers. Everything had a musty smell and the dust that came with them made his nose tingle.

No booze, though.

'Come on, come on!' Dean breathed. He fished out some of the paper wedges hoping that they masked a bottle of something he could welcome with an open throat.

The age of the papers made the newest item stand out. It was a small card that Dean picked up and read with a degree of despair.

The card was a sedate brown, but the words upon it may as well have been written in flashing neon.

The words said: *Alcoholics Anonymous.*

'Oh, Harold,' Dean said to the man in the photograph. 'How could you be so stupid?'

In his head, Jenna started chuckling.

* * *

Dean fought off a wave of despondency. It should have consumed him, but one small concept prevented him from going under.

The success rate for beating alcohol addiction was poor. Dean looked at the more recent pictures on the desk. Harold had the same look in his eyes. The face was aged and the dark hair had blanched, but those eye told stories.

'Harold,' Dean said, 'you've been a naughty boy, haven't you?'

Harold, of course, said nothing.

'So where is it?' Dean said, turning away from the desk. 'One apartment, two separate lives. Drink did the do, didn't it, Harold? Destroyed whatever old Maud saw in you. You tried but you couldn't stop. So all I have to do is find it.'

Instinctively, Dean's gaze went back to the bedrooms as he revisited an old article he'd written on sobriety. Men were lazy hoarders. He doubted Harold would be any different. Vodka was the clandestine drink of choice as it could be inconspicuously added to the most innocuous substances, water or squash, for example.

Dean raced to the first bedroom and peered in again. It had a dressing table with a large mirror. A hair brush and a leather jewellery box were sitting on it.

'Not in your room, Maud,' Dean said, and went next door where he found a half bottle of *Smirnoff Black* tucked inside a brown loafer at the back of Harold's wardrobe.

Dean drank it in three swallows while still on his hands and knees, savouring the fire the liquor put in his throat and guts. He received it greedily like a man pounded down water after having spent days lost in the desert.

Dean turned over onto his backside and rested against the bed. He sighed long and hard, and the contented sound was good for another few seconds had it not been curtailed by a sudden and totally unwelcome event.

Coming from the direction of the front door was the unmistakable noise of shuffling feet. He clambered out of the room, his only concern to make sure that another living soul had somehow made it through the night without succumbing to the madness that was now the city.

Seconds before he'd snorted down a quarter bottle of vodka he would have thought twice, or perhaps even considered the possibility that whoever had come into Harold and Maud's apartment might not be here with the best of intentions. But the booze was steering the boat and the rocks were not to register until Dean saw the thing clutching the doorway as he exited the bedroom and turned into the hall.

It might have been Harold. The blood and holes in its cheeks made identification difficult. Its eyes were jaundiced, twin yellow orbs, shocking in their sockets. They flitted to him and locked on. The sleeve of a plum-coloured suit and the shirt beneath had been ripped off and revealed a bare arm that had sustained so many bites to it the flesh appeared undulated.

'Oh, my God.' Dean's words came as a hiss.

The thing in the doorway hissed back at Dean, its mouth hanging open and blood oozing from it like strings of red liquorice.

'Okay,' Dean said holding his hands out to placate the creature as it came towards him. 'Let's not be too hasty, now, fella.'

The shape ran at him, the din from its mouth coming as a thin scream that broke apart as liquid poured down its throat. It was a vicious and feral sound, the kind that meant there was no reasoning with it, only flight before *that mouth* went to work.

Dean ran back into the lounge, the creature following close behind. Something traced across his back and he realised he'd managed to stay ahead of an outstretched hand.

Dean went down on one knee as his foot slipped on a Persian rug. Fate was putting in a brief appearance before pissing off again, no doubt. As Dean went down, the thing chasing him continued at speed and couldn't stop. Its feet struck Dean's lower back and it flew headlong into the veranda window. The whole frame shuddered as the reinforced glass took the hit. The nets parted and a spider-web crack rippled out from the point where the head made contact. As though a switch had been thrown, the body collapsed and lay still; the only evidence of its activity remained in a bloody smear upon the net curtains.

Dean moved, heading for the landing. Enough was enough. He had some booze on board and now he had to get back to his place and take stock.

'You need to plan,' he muttered. 'And the first part is to get the fuck out of this apartment.'

Dean reached the front door, intending to go left back to his home. It might not have any booze, but it didn't have any slavering humanoids either, so it got the deal. He pulled up short when he saw the shape silhouetted against the open door of his apartment. It was malformed, as buckled and twisted as the drawer on old Maud's kitchen worktop.

Another thing. It had its back to him. Somehow it had wandered past and made for his sanctuary.

'Great.'

He considered his options: stay at Harold and Maud's place, where the booze was gone and there was a body that may or may not get back up again, or head right and take his chances on another floor or out in the streets.

All things being equal, waiting things out at the Marshalls' was fast becoming the best meal on a shitty menu.

Up until he heard the crash behind him, Dean was all but closing the door. He had time to look back and see a shape staggering around in the lounge and an overturned occasional table. Fear took him out into the corridor where he inadvertently planted a foot onto the minced corpse lying on the floor. There was the hideous sound of snapping bones and a loud fart of escaping gas.

Dean didn't wait around to see if his mishap had made him the focus of attention, he merely extrapolated himself from the corpse's innards and bolted towards the elevators.

He used the winking elevator waiting lights as a guide in the gloom, the walls as stability. The corridor opened out into a small landing where the elevator doors waited wide and inviting. Dean could immediately see- and smell - that he wasn't alone.

Several still, twisted shapes lay in the gloom. Arms and legs rose like the frigid undergrowth of some dark and evil forest. He used the walls to circumvent these terrible obstacles until he made it to the elevator car. Inside, the overheads flickered, turning the maimed body inside into a shimmering freak show.

It was Harold Marshall; Dean gleaned that much from the lifeless eyes staring at him. The rest of Marshall's face was ravaged with gaping wounds and teeth marks. His throat had been torn out, and his nose was nothing more than a gaping hole.

The horror of it took a back seat. Before he realised what he was doing, Dean was going through the pockets of a long raincoat the unfortunate Marshall had been wearing at the time he was savaged.

In seconds, Dean found the two half-bottles of vodka and a silver hip flask. One bottle was nearly empty and Dean finished the job without hesitation. Then he unscrewed the second bottle and took two huge gulps. Part of him wanted and needed more, but survival these days worked on many levels. He showed restraint in the absence of any more booze. He stowed the remaining bottle and the hip flask in the back of his jeans pockets, and grabbed Marshall's ankles. Numbed by the vodka, he kept his revulsion in check as he dragged the hapless, lifeless drunk from the elevator car.

Pots and kettles, Deano, Jenna sniped. *Pots and kettles.*

'Fuck you,' he said as he stepped into the car. He hit the ground floor button and waited for the door to close on the horror.

And waited.

Not far away, footfalls and snarls came from the direction of his apartment.

The elevator doors remained steadfast. Dean reached for the button again and stabbed at the plastic discs, not caring what floor he ended up on as long as it wasn't here.

The snarls had become growls, low and guttural, as though a tiger roamed the floors. Dean concluded he'd probably have more luck evading a tiger. It was no use, the elevators were fucked. He had to use the stairs and eased himself from the car, not seeing much in the murk, but a shimmering fire exit sign called him on. Again he followed the contours of the walls until he reached the fire escape and the stairs behind the thick doors.

Hands slapped against walls as the creatures hunting him in the dark tried to steer their way through the carnage. But as he managed to slip into the stairway, their growls were still some way off.

The emergency lighting overhead bathed the stairwell in a creamy glow, making it a significant contrast to the landing he'd left behind. He ran down the steps, pulling free the vodka bottle and stopping only to empty it before moving on. He discarded the bottle on the stairs and felt the touch of its contents, welcoming it like an old ally in the sudden and uncertain war that was now called *staying alive*.

After several flights of stairs, Dean reached the foyer. He gently opened the door and looked out. The compact space was made smaller by the wreckage. The reception area had been devastated. Chairs were overturned, plant pots had been smashed; their terracotta shells and swatches of dirt strewn about the black-and-white tiled floor. The counter had several holes punched into it and, lying upon it, the body of the concierge which had acquired his fair share of damage, too.

There were three more corpses between Dean and the entrance. As with those he'd encountered before, their flesh had been mauled and the blood that had jetted across the foyer lay congealed in oval pools of black tar.

Dean moved towards the double doors, both slabs of heavy security glass, breath waving against the tea towel as he went. The air was heavy with the familiar sweet stink of decaying flesh. His gaze flitted as he sought out new dangers in an already perilous scene.

Dean made it to the entrance, his journey marked by tacky, bloody footprints. At the doors, he placed a hand against the glass as he heard running footsteps.

A figure flashed by, a blur behind the pane, and Dean stepped back for a second. The figure disappeared and the footfalls receded. Dean dropped the tea towel away from his face and pushed at the doors, his intention to check all was clear.

He'd only opened the door a few inches when a sudden shape blocked the light and a blood-smeared hand shot through the gap and grabbed the collar of his shirt. He yanked backwards in an attempt to break free, but the strength and determination from his assailant was too powerful.

With a yelp, Dean Sharp was dragged out onto the street, and found out first-hand just how much of Hell had come to Earth.

* * *

As Dean fell out through the door his attacker lost its grip on him. He went spinning onto the pavement, the hard concrete skinning both knees and making him cry out. His protestations were lost among the clamouring din about him. Snarls and screams mingled with the dull thud of explosions and the insistent wails of sirens and car alarms. It was Bedlam three times over and, adding to it all, was the acrid stench of burning flesh.

His assailant, a small woman in her forties, had brown tousled hair and a face that twisted into a pink mask. Her eyes were cold and misted with a familiar yellow haze. She wore the tattered remnants of a traffic warden uniform; the torn jacket revealing a white blouse smeared in some brown substance that reeked of fish.

The woman was on Dean in seconds, and knocked him backwards. He landed heavily, his spine hitting the asphalt. He yelled with pain and fear as she scrambled over him, straddling him, with her skirt hitching over torn black stockings that revealed mottled legs with livid red weals. Her hands found his throat again and the grip was like a car clamp pinching off his airway.

Something came to him through the fog of panic.

Don't push, Deano, pull!

He remembered a personal safety exercise he'd attended after being assaulted by someone he'd been investigating who hadn't taken kindly to the press rooting through their trash. Perhaps Lady Luck had invited him into her embrace for a while and he was going to accept the offer wholesale.

Dean reached up and cupped the warden's right elbow with both his hands, locking out the arm. She was bearing down on him, her jaw opening slightly wider than it really should. He bent his right leg and used it to power his hip upwards and sideways while pulling on the elbow with both hands.

The warden flew in an oblique arc as Dean rolled in the opposite direction and sprang to his feet. He was in time to see her bouncing off of a lamp post, the left leg folding beneath her and snapping with the report of a pistol shot. But she didn't scream out or curse in agony. Instead, she pushed herself up onto her feet using the very leg she'd just shattered. Her gait was swaggering, the leg protesting by turning into a Z shape when she bore down upon it.

In panic, Dean ran back to his building and a terrible realisation came to him. The door was self-locking and key coded. The number ran for cover in his bewildered brain.

'What's the code, Dean?' he said urgently. 'Think, damn it!'

The woman kept coming for him, the bones of her ruined femur grating together with a noise like sandpaper against plywood.

Seven, eight, three, six.

He punched at the key pad and waited for the buzzer to tell him he hadn't fucked it up.

No such buzzer came.

He tried again, this time switching the last two digits.

Nothing. No buzzer. Just the dragging and shuffling of a leg that shouldn't be able to move at all.

He concentrated on the key pad, trying to ignore the shadow that was beginning to stretch out on the pavement, a shadow with a leg in the shape of a Z and arms reaching out.

'You can remember this drunk, for fuck's sake,' he cursed as he reversed the first two digits and pressed in the code. There was a drawn out hiss at his shoulder and flecks of spittle peppered his neck.

The lock buzzed loudly. He pulled open the door and squeezed into the smallest of gaps he could create. Hands grabbed at the material of his shirt as he moved; the cotton collar tore away with a purr.

Dean found the door handle and hauled it shut using all of his body weight in order to achieve the manoeuvre. He collapsed inside the foyer, gasping for air. It didn't matter that it was stale, dank, and coated with the smell of rotting meat. His lungs sucked it in with the gratitude of a drowning man pulled onto the deck of a lifeboat.

He climbed to his feet and stepped away from the glass. In a mixture of horror and fascination, he watched the figure looking back at him. The warden's mouth licked and slathered against the pane, leaving a veil of saliva and blood. As Dean watched her biting against the window, his eyes moistened with horror and sadness.

'Jesus,' he whispered. 'What have we become?' He reached into his jeans and allowed the contents of the hip flask to give him comfort.

TEN YEARS AGO

The bar was small and reeked of stale beer and cigarettes.

Dean sat at a corner table peeling back the skein of a beer mat as he watched local bowery bums sitting on bar stools and talking bullshit about football and horse racing.

It's the language of the mentally languid, he remembered Jenna saying once. He recalled it as one of the few times he actually agreed with her.

In his breast pocket, his cell phone kicked in and the buzz hardened his left nipple. He looked at the screen and took a swig from his pint of lager before answering.

'Sharp,' he announced into the moulded silver Nokia.

'Where the fuck are you?' Alan Cound, his editor, had a bullish nature at the best of times. Today his voice had an even crisper tone as irritation whittled its edges.

'That's a trick question, right?' Dean sighed.

'Perceptive,' Cound said. 'I got a job for you.'

'I'm on leave,' Dean pointed out.

'Sick leave,' Cound corrected him. 'To sort out your problem?'

'Yeah,' Dean muttered.

'Well, I'll take the sick leave request as seriously as you are,' Cound said. 'I want you to go to Gullcrest.'

'Why?'

'You know why,' Cound said. 'Susan Hadley.'

Dean lifted his glass and took a series of heavy swallows. He wiped his mouth with his hand then said, 'Susan Hadley, six years old, disappeared eighteen months ago. Missing, presumed drowned, according to the official reports. In reality, no one has a fucking clue.'

'What are you? A talking journal?' Cound sniped. 'Yes, THAT Susan Hadley.'

'The girl's gone. The investigation, cold,' he said into his mobile. 'The police found nothing at the time, despite a national appeal and hundreds of man hours. What the hell chance do I have?'

'The place got cluttered,' Cound said. 'Police, our lot, the whole fucking world had eyes on that village at the time. Things get missed, Dean. Things *got* missed.'

'How would you know that?' Dean said.

'I was there recently,' Cound said carefully 'With Jodi.'

'Jodi?' Dean spluttered. 'The model?'

'Yeah, the model,' Cound snapped. 'I was with her this weekend. At Gullcrest.'

'Gullcrest?' Dean couldn't hide his surprise.

'You a fuckin' parrot now?' Cound said. 'We stopped by there on the way to her place in Cornwall. We got talking about the Hadley girl, and we stayed the night in the local hotel.'

'Too much information.' Dean chuckled.

'You're a real comedian, Sharp,' Cound said. 'Lee Evans must be shitting himself. You listen and listen well. I sensed something when I was there, something wrong. You get me?'

'As wrong as the thought of you and nineteen-year-old glamour model?' Dean mused.

'I'll let you have that one,' Cound said. 'Another crack like it, I'll be calling you in to fire your pissed-up arse after I kick it across the newsroom.'

'Yeah,' Dean said, reaching for his cigarettes. He hooked the phone under his chin as he sparked up.

'So, I go to Gullcrest 'cause you think the place feels wrong,' he said after blowing blue smoke. 'It's a small village, a close-knit community. A tragedy like the Hadley girl is going to leave scars. Maybe they're still grieving. And you're just sensing it.'

'No,' Cound said. 'People were eyeballing me like some pariah. It's like they knew who I was. It's more than that, I'm sure of it.'

'Even if there is, what's the point?' Dean asked. 'I mean, this will just rake up old ground. The residents of Gullcrest already hate the press. They blame us for shitting in their yard. No one will talk to me.'

A long pause followed and Dean recognised it for what it was; Cound trying to find the angle - the hook - to draw him in.

'I remember when you first came to the paper,' he said.

'Oh, fuck, don't pull that shit,' Dean interjected, but Cound continued regardless.

'Yeah, you sat in front of me, as green as grass, and told me what you wanted to achieve in life,' he said. 'You remember that, Dean? Do you?'

'Yeah.'

'A chance to make a difference, right a few wrongs,' Cound said. 'I'm presuming this hasn't changed? I'm assuming you haven't lost the taste for a story…the thirst for a Pulitzer?'

'There's no story here,' Dean protested.

'What's the matter with you, man? There's always a story,' Cound insisted. 'I sensed it when I was there not three days ago. You're the paper's investigative journalist. I'm the editor. And as the editor I'm telling you to go and fucking investigate! We clear?'

'You're the boss,' Dean said, his voice heavy with resignation.

'You got that right,' Cound said.

They hung up.

* * *

The MR2 pulled onto the drive of the Olde Majestic Hotel, its passage marked by the crunch of gravel beneath Goodyear tyres.

The building lived up to the brochure, an impressive sight; grey bricks were draped in climbing ivy, the broad leaves covering some of the Dornier windows. At four storeys high, the hotel was topped by ramparts, where crows perched and cawed loudly. A series of flags, emblazoned with advertising logos and pseudo heraldry, fluttered in the breeze coming in from the beachhead in the east.

Behind the steering wheel, Dean chewed his lip as he drove the car through a lichgate that gave way to a small car park. Several other vehicles languished in the shade of three huge oak trees. The summer sun was confident overhead, giving the whitewashed gravel such a dazzling glow it had Dean reaching for his sunglasses as he climbed out of the car.

The Olde Majestic Hotel had been recommended by Cound after the gregarious editor had taken his rotund belly and ultra-slim squeeze into its auspices for a dirty weekend. Jodi - aka: Jennifer Bennett - was usually seen between the sheets of their tabloid paper. Dean was now aware that Cound had enough clout to see Jodi between the sheets of the Olde Majestic Hotel. All of this on the paper's expense account as Mrs Cound was holed up in some spa or other in Sussex.

Dean shuddered at the thought he may end up in a room, a bed, in which his boss had banged the latest model on their books. The image was enough for his face to pull into a grimace as he went to the boot to retrieve his suitcase.

He'd travelled light: two pairs of jeans, a thin jacket, assorted underwear and a nose for a story, even one as stale as the Susan Hadley affair. It was all he needed to get by these days. Oh, and Ol' Jim, of course. Two bottles of the liquor languished in the green Stagg trolley suitcase. Ol' Jim was his only consistent travel companion and when he wasn't around he was sorely missed.

Dean pulled the case free of the boot and extended the handle ready to pull it towards the hotel. Overhead, seagulls wheeled as white V shapes in the clear sky, their cries mingling with the soothing shush of the nearby ocean.

After locking the car, Dean followed the signs steering him back through the lichgate and up to a small path, made dark by the honeysuckle entwined on a trestle archway.

He found the tunnel claustrophobic, and fought against thoughts of suffocation and devils lurking in gloomy corners; childhood nightmares that never seemed content just to leave him be. They weren't even monsters of his creation, they were Jenna's handiwork. The result of one evening left alone with Frankenstein's daughter and a prank to get a young Dean locked under the stairs while his sister told him dark stories of demons stealing away his breath. He'd screamed himself hoarse before she'd let him out. The event lasted for twenty minutes max, but its impact was to remain for a lifetime. Ol' Jim was always there to hold his hand, these days. Dean felt his ally's calming presence as he walked down the passageway, but it was still with a sense of restrained relief that, after a few moments, a series of yellow stone steps came into view.

At the top of the steps stood a huge door made from rich yellow wood and glass, crowned with the banner, *Reception*. He dragged his trolley case up the steps and entered the lobby, taking in the sights and sounds of a remote seaside hotel as he made his way to the reception desk.

Several large rugs, each richly decorated in paisley or fleur de leys motifs, covered worn, dark floor boards. Two beaten-up, brown Chesterfield sofas sat at a right angle opposite an open, but unlit, fireplace crafted from Portland stone.

Although the central features were Regency period, this did not extend to the rest of the lobby. Paintings and wallpaper were Art Deco, and the reception desk was set back and staffed by an elderly woman in a bright red tabard finished with golden braid and brass buttons. She peered over the top of half-moon glasses as Dean approached.

'Good afternoon,' she said, stepping to her left where Dean noticed the reservation sheet. On her ample bosom, her brass name badge told Dean her name was Alison Defu.

'Hi,' Dean replied. 'I have a room booked under the name of Sharp.'

Defu scanned the book, a blue pen in her chipolata fingers. Her cheeks were as red as the tabard she wore. She finally tapped her pen against a line of scrawl.

'Here we are,' she said. 'Dean Sharp?'

'Yes, that's the one.'

She looked up from the book and scrutinised his face with eyes that were as blue as they were shrewd. 'Says here that it is an open reservation?'

'Yes,' Dean said. 'Is that a problem?'

'Not at all,' Defu smiled. 'Gullcrest is a fishing village. People are usually passing through on their way to Land's End. Not many choose to stay any longer than a night or two. What brings you here?'

This caught Dean off guard but he recovered well. The question was a gift.

'I'm a writer.' It was almost dismissive, as though it should mean nothing at all. By design, of course. People were more receptive to the term writer; a stark contrast to that of a reporter. Dean had learned this a while ago. Even flowered with professional terms such as *investigative journalist*, it didn't keep at bay the suspicious and contemptuous response from the general public.

'We tend to attract them,' Defu said. 'Especially mystery writers.'

His heart stalled. Without, he gave off an air of nonchalance.

'What do you mean?' He searched her face for subterfuge but didn't see any lurking there.

'Just the setting,' Defu said as she began the checking-in procedure by passing him a form to complete. 'The coves around here have a mystique all of their own. Tend to get those creative juices flowing, eh?'

'I guess so,' Dean said as he filled out his form.

'So do you?' Defu pressed.

'What?'

'Write mysteries?' she explained.

'Yes,' he confirmed but failed to elaborate. Defu showed interest and Dean had to figure a few things out.

Firstly, was her interest born from a position as the community vanguard, checking out newcomers so as to protect the integrity of her village? Or was she genuinely intrigued by his presence here? He could work on the latter; it would be an inroad to ascertain if Cound, at least, was right in his suspicions and Dean might get his story after all. If Defu was the vanguard then Cound's suspicions that something was amiss would be confirmed but little else would come of it.

These were the dilemmas he would have to navigate before he could get down to the detail. In this case, the detail had a name and a memory that would never die in all those who knew it.

If not, well Dean would go with a gnawing suspicion that his editor could see nothing more in the eyes of those in Gullcrest than general curiosity as to how a fifty-year-old Teletubby could net a glamour model. He tried not to smile at the thought.

'So what have you written?' Defu asked. 'I might have read it.'

'Oh, I've self-published an e-book,' he said quickly. 'I'm doing research for the next.'

'Self-published?' she repeated. 'E-book?'

The interest died in her eyes and part of him, the part that didn't want this to end as soon as it began, was happy to see its demise.

'Well,' she said dourly, 'enjoy your stay with us. Breakfast is served until nine-thirty. Dinner is seven until ten.'

'Do you have a bar?'

'It closes at eleven,' she said.

'Care to point out where it is?' he asked.

'Don't you want to be shown to your room?' Defu appeared confused.

'Plenty of time for that,' he said.

* * *

'You drink like there's no tomorrow, lad.'

Dean observed the barman. A counter made of black wood separated them and a row of spent shot glasses carved their mark into its ebony surface like a glacier slipping across the surface of Earth.

'Always does though, doesn't it?' Dean replied.

'Huh?' The barman cocked his head and his grey eyes seemed reluctant to leave Dean's whiskey-slack face.

'Tomorrow,' Dean explained. 'Always does come, right?'

'Not for everyone,' the barman said. The whiskey had taken the edge off the anxiety but Dean was still alert, still probing for an inroad.

Something sad and rueful held court in the barman's eyes for a fleeting moment before moving on.

'What's your name?' Dean asked.

'What's yours?' Rueful had decamped and suspicion was setting up a tent.

'Dean.'

'Reginald,' the barman said. 'Reginald Grimes.'

Grimes ran his fingers through hair that was a blend of white and blonde. The lights built into the bar frame made the brow exposed by his receding hairline glisten like sunlight hitting steel. Dean saw something in Grimes's demeanour. He'd seen it countless times in people who tried to keep the lid on a great trauma. Every now and then, pain wanted to boil over and sully the hob. For the first time since Cound had made the call, Dean was not so dismissive of his editor's assumptions about Gullcrest's bleak past.

Sure, time had moved on since the Hadley girl had disappeared, but at its passing it seemed as though people might have held onto the pain a little too long and it was beginning to cripple their lives. Based on his experiences of interviewing many victims of many terrible things, this meant a lot to Dean.

It meant that, far from hiding behind a wall of silence, some might be ready to stand the guards down for a while. And, inside the Trojan Horse, Dean would be waiting patiently for the right moment.

'What brings you to Gullcrest?' Grimes said as he transferred the glasses from the bar to the dishwasher beneath.

'Writer,' Dean said. It was convincing enough to have Grimes nodding. He gave the barman the same spiel as he dumped on Defu. It was partially true, of course, though some recipients of Dean's articles may have thought that 'writing' was the last descriptor they'd use. Besides, consistency was deceit's ally, and no doubt the staff here talked to each other about the guests.

'Always wanted to write a story,' Grimes said.

'They say everyone has a book in them,' Dean offered. Cliché worked best in bars. Dean had been in enough to know that as a fact.

What would you write, Reg? Would you document your memories of that time when a little girl, a symbol of hope for the future, was snatched away from this quaint little village? Would you scratch your pain and woe upon the paper and wish that hope might return someday and give light to the darkness in your heart? Would you let me look upon your private thoughts made real in ink on vellum sheets, scrutinise them for clues as to what really happened here?

A sudden burst of laughter shook Dean from his internal inquiry. The merriment came from two youths who had just entered the bar. Their shadows played upon the glasses on the counter as they passed by.

'Evenin', lads,' Grimes said to the newcomers. 'The usual?'

'Cheers, Reg,' said one of the youths. He was tall and stick-thin, and his limbs were bulked out by a combat jacket that looked to Dean as though it might have seen actual service at some point in its life. On the lapel was a badge denoting the band, *Nirvana*.

'Here for the evenin', Rob?' Grimes asked the kid in the combat jacket.

'Three guesses,' Rob said as he scratched at a black goatee. 'You're a real joker, Reg. What do you think, Paul?'

'I think I'd better go home and get my mum to stitch my sides back together,' said the smaller youth. His mousey blond hair was an untidy thatch and he wore a *Pearl Jam* T-shirt. His combat pants had so many pockets it took him a while to find his wallet. 'There's nowhere else to go in this deadbeat town.'

'Nowhere that'll serve you two, more like,' Grimes said as he poured two pints of lager. The youths said nothing, a testament to the accuracy of the barman's statement.

Dean watched his reflection in the mirror across the bar. To anyone looking in, he would have seemed like just another journeyman taking refreshment from yet another hostelry, but as he listened to the harmless banter, he sensed nothing but opportunity to kick-start the search for Susan Hadley.

* * *

His hotel room reflected the regency and Art Deco hybrid of the foyer. The walls were adorned with bold prints and reproductions of Rene Lalique and Leon Bakst paintings. The furniture, with its deep redwoods and Olde English designs, fostered the ongoing sense of incongruence.

This mattered little to Dean. He left his suitcase in a recess where redundant clothes hangers were hooked in a regimented line on a single brass rail. His clothes would remain in the case, but Dean was always going to keep Ol' Jim close by, on his bedside table in fact, two bottles standing proud like sentinels keeping reality at bay. What was reality these days? It was a thought he was always mulling over in the quieter times.

Susan Hadley? Was she reality? Or just another ghost he had to chase on behalf of his boss?

He was unscrewing the bottle so that Ol' Jim could contribute to the debate when his mobile began to purr on the bedside cupboard.

He reached for it and hit the 'answer call' key, expecting to hear Cound demand an update.

'Dean?'

Fuck it. It was Jenna.

'What do you want?' Dean made no attempt to hide his resentment. He'd given up on such pretence a while ago.

'Guess?'

'I quit playing your games when I left home,' he said. 'Get to the point.'

'We need to discuss the other day,' she clarified. 'What you said to Dad.' Her voice was harsh and unyielding.

Corporate.

'All I did was thank him for making me the man I am today,' Dean said.

'You called him a self-pitying drunk,' Jenna said.

'Yeah,' Dean said after taking a swig of Ol' Jim. 'That just about covers it.'

'You need to apologise,' she said. 'He's devastated.'

'Truth tends to sting a bit.' Dean's tone was nonchalant but anger was stomping through the tranquillity like a petulant teenager with an X-Box ban. 'But you had to be me to really get it.'

'Dad did the best he could, you ungrateful pig.' Jenna snorted in contempt. 'After Mum died -'

'After Mum died life went to shit,' Dean growled. 'I was raised by a drunk and a bitch and I don't want anything to do with either. Fuck-bye, Jenna.'

He killed the call and tossed the phone onto the bed. Within seconds it was buzzing again.

Dean went to it and switched the device off. Breathing heavily, he wiped his brow with a trembling hand and brought back his resolve with two gulps from his bottle of whisky.

He flopped onto the bed and allowed his temper to ease down on the gas. As sleep snuggled up to him, he found that any contentment nature's sedative brought to him was to be short-lived.

The dream made sure of it.

* * *

The commotion outside made the small, cobbled streets echo. The sound of heavy boots and sharp cries of anguish lifted high into the air where they were snatched away by the gale.

The bulbous black clouds spat fat raindrops onto the vehicles below, the thick thud of the droplets as they slapped against the bodywork adding to the commotion.

Dean looked on as the three silver people carriers disgorged many figures, their white biochem suits and black gas masks making them look like faceless ghosts as they spilled out onto the pavement.

The group grappled with a small, writhing figure - a young girl - who called out to them, pleading with those who pinned her arms and legs, to let her go. The shapes were telling her to be quiet, to calm the fuck down, it was all for her own good, for her own protection. But it was of little use, the girl was too distraught. For a moment, her face turned in Dean's direction, her pale skin moist with rainwater as it cascaded down her cheeks.

Susan Hadley's eyes met his, tears lost among the rain drops. They held him- implored him - to help her. He stood transfixed. The girl's eyes were like a twin sunrise under the halogen street lamps; twin yellow orbs sparkling in the rain as it streaked from the sky.

An arm broke free, a small hand rose from the melee, and in her tiny fingers, Susan held aloft a slip of paper. Her fingers opened and the wind snatched the slip away from her. It was ruffled and buffeted, spiralling in each blast of wet air, but Dean knew it was destined to reach him, to land at his feet where he saw the digits written upon it in thick black letters:

Eight, eight, one, eight.

A thin scream made him look back towards the scuffle.

From his refuge in the rain-lashed shadows, Dean watched as Susan Hadley was bundled into the lead people carrier and three of her captors piled into the vehicle.

As the car wheelspun and took off at speed, Dean's eyes were seared by a huge flash of lightning and the world turned frost-white for a few seconds. As monochrome returned to Technicolor, the assault on Dean's senses left him panting for breath.

The cobbled street was gone, replaced by the hotel driveway. It was still dark, but the sodium lights poured rich, luminous pools on the chaos outside the Olde Majestic. A writhing mass of people, too many to count, were pounding each other, tearing away flesh in thick chunks, the blood black under the lamps.

Dean watched transfixed as one woman in her seventies launched herself at a youth, head bowed, and caught the boy square in his face. Blood gushed from his broken nose and he screamed, not in pain but feral, brutal rage. He grabbed the woman by the shoulder and threw her to the ground. She tried to stand, hissing through a set of dislodged dentures. The boy brought down his foot; a heavy walking boot caved in her sternum. The youth continued to stamp on the flailing body until his ankle was awash with her innards and blood plumed from her mouth like some macabre fountain in time with his foot. Her teeth finally lost their place and slopped onto the gravel, their grin gory and eternal.

Dean remained riveted; his gaze not able to pull away, such was the nature of dreams. Even if he had been able to shut out the slaughter going on before him, his brain reverberated with the terrible, guttural sounds that came along for the ride.

There were also the eyes, of course; yellow eyes that appeared like fireflies in the blackness. Even in his dream state, Dean was drawn into them, mesmerised by the inference that all of this was skewed and relentlessly vivid, even for a dream. Even as an unexpected, searing light exploded in the sky, erasing his vision, a screaming thought cleaved the image and Dean was awake in his room at the Olde Majestic Hotel, his skin moist, his breathing ragged.

While the terrible images began to burrow into the depths of his subconscious like some vile creature shying away from daylight, the thought that had dragged him from his nightmare intended to linger a while.

He climbed from his bed and went to the bathroom, where he threw cold water onto the ashen expression staring back at him in the mirror. All the time, the errant thought swirled about his brain.

If this was just a dream, why did it feel like it was something closer to a memory?

* * *

Dean had drawn a conclusion as soon as he'd seen the teenagers at the bar. It was a simple premise, that of the disaffected youth and their alienation from the older generation. Dean had first stirred the idea when he saw the Nirvana pin on Rob's jacket. Cobain was a voice for youth culture and the banner was loud and proud: Don't trust anyone over twenty. The two lads were underage drinkers; Reg's comment about not being able to drink anywhere else inferred as much.

Through Grimes, Dean recognised that those who remembered Susan Hadley enough to give a shit were unlikely to talk. Rob and Paul after a few pints of free beer might prove to be a different story, tell a different story. They would've known the girl, known her friends. It was a loose theory but one he intended to test all the same. The adage 'stir the pot and see what comes to the surface' rang true and he intended to grab the ladle with both hands. All he needed to do was draw upon his ability to be patient and wait twenty-four hours.

The moment came around very quickly. Such was the time machine called alcoholism.

* * *

The following evening, Dean ate dinner early. The dining room was large and its low ceiling had exposed oak beams that broke the surface of the plaster like skeletal ribs pressing against the belly of some starving beast. Dean had an Old English fillet, cooked rare with creamed potatoes and seasonal vegetables. His starter and dessert consisted of Ol' Jim.

Throughout his meal he intermittently scanned his wristwatch for the time. Rob and Paul would be in the bar at seven thirty. Dean knew enough about pub culture to recognise a regular, and such a title wasn't an award handed out on a whim, it was an ethic. Same pub, same time, so the wino world turned.

He finished his meal and took up his spot at the bar. The plan was simple enough: he would use their routine to ambush them, their poison to bait the trap. Rob and Paul would collect their illicit drinks and saunter over to their table. Dean planned to wait at the bar until the youths had finished their second pint then he'd do his thing just before they stepped up for a third. No one here was going to pass on a free drink; underage Rob and Paul would be no exception. The beer would be his entrance fee to their world and he planned to spend his time there wisely.

There were four other people in the bar who were keeping Grimes busy. Two men in smart, albeit slightly dishevelled, business suits— the attire of salesmen passing through in the chase for another commission - and an elderly couple who wore matching beige body warmers. The couple, a man who may have had stature before gravity began calling the shots, had shocking white hair and a knobbly walking stick made from yellow wood. His partner was a small woman who sipped her tall drink - gin and tonic with ice and a slice - with the trepidation of a deer taking a draught in a river clearing during hunting season.

Part of Dean's interest in journalism had come from his fascination with people and the stories they carried with them. He found watching strangers interact, either with others or the environment in which they found themselves, was better than anything the TV networks could concoct in the name of entertainment.

The familiar sound of Rob and Paul laughing merrily brought him back to the here and now. Theirs was a contrived entrance, a statement to those present that they belonged, so no need to question it, camouflage in plain sight.

Dean tipped the lads a nod and they reciprocated as the ritual played out. Grimes made casual banter and poured their drinks, Paul paid for the first round after checking his pockets for thirty seconds. The hands on the clock above the bar, and the actors in the scene, all went through the motions until the youths were sat at their table, hunched across from each other and talking shit.

Dean sipped his whisky and watched the events unfurl. By the time Paul had stood ready for the third pint, Dean was already reaching for a twenty pound note in his back pocket.

* * *

'Anyways, my old man said, "Ye'll need a good breakfast inside ye, lad. Ye'll be needin' something to throw up as ye cut that ol' bitch open!" Can you believe that?'

As Rob told his story, Paul slapped his hands on the table and guffawed loudly. Dean sat between them and chuckled, playing his part as he let the booze do the rest.

Rob was talking about life as the son of a fisherman. His dad owned a small boat known as the Mary Jane, the name of Rob's grandmother. For more than five decades, his dad had fished in the waters off of Gullcrest's coastline. The fact that Rob was discussing the details of the first time he'd been asked to gut a tuna fish was testament to the inroads Dean had made during the course of the evening. This was made even more remarkable when Dean considered Paul.

The alcohol had helped the youth open up, too. Gone was his timid, almost perplexed demeanour. It had been replaced by an easy-going kid, who was happy to talk about the loss of parents in a car accident when he was six, and his subsequent fractured life in a children's home that had given him rudimentary comfort, if not security, for eleven of the seventeen years he had been on Earth.

'So why do you lads come here?' Dean asked. 'There must be places in town geared for kids of your age.'

'There's fuck-all in town for anyone under a hundred, mate.' Rob chuckled.

'It does seem a quiet town,' Dean agreed.

'Eh? A quiet town?' Paul said incredulously. 'That's like saying super storm Sandy left a few puddles.'

'So nothing ever happens here?' Dean said. Inside he was getting ready to make his move.

'Nothing,' conceded Rob. 'It's a dead zone.'

'Anything *ever* happened, anything out of the ordinary?' Dean pressed, fighting the urge to lean forward and give away anything other than cursory interest.

'There was Susan Hadley,' Rob said.

'Who?' Dean's heart jittered for a few seconds before getting its act together.

'You mean you don't know about that?' Paul said. 'A kid who disappeared. A while ago now. It was all over the TV.'

'Hell, I spent most of the past few years pissed. I wouldn't have known a TV report from feckin' *Sesame Street*.' Dean's lie was smooth, the culmination of years of working with the best liars in the industry. 'No surprise I missed it. So what happened?'

Rob told Dean nothing that he didn't already know. Susan Hadley was reported last seen on the small promenade, looking out to sea. It was on the same day that a north-westerly gale had decided to hit the coastline. The sea was angry and spent a few hours delivering blows. The person who had reported seeing Susan as the waves pounded in was an off-duty police officer who was so consumed with guilt he'd eaten both barrels of a twelve bore a year later.

'Fascinating,' Dean said, though, in reality, he was frustrated at the lack of new information.

Until Paul interjected.

He said three words, and the conversation stalled for a few seconds as Dean digested them.

'I'm sorry?' Dean said to buy some time. 'I didn't quite catch that.'

'I saw her,' Paul said again. 'On the day they said she disappeared. I saw her.'

Surprise showed on Rob's face. This was new information to all parties. Booze had no respect for secrets, especially those that were only inches beneath the surface.

'Why didn't you say something?' Rob asked. Dean suspected this question had broad scope, a query from one friend to another.

Paul thought this through for a few moments. When he did reply it was tentative, as though he wasn't quite sure of its validity in the here and now.

'Everyone was saying Susan disappeared from the promenade. Drowned, they said,' he muttered into his pint glass. 'Who'd believe me, a kid from care who'd broken his curfew?'

You didn't want to get into deep shit. You would've been the last person to see her alive and that was a lake of shit in which you didn't want to drown.

'So what did you see?' Dean asked.

'I was out on the bluff,' he explained. 'I like it there when storms hit. Makes me feel free, if y'get me?'

'Sure,' Dean said.

'Anyways, the bluff looks down on the beach and I thought I saw something outside the entrance to Cooper's Cove. It was only for a few seconds. I couldn't believe anyone could be out there. The waves were fucking up the cove big time.' He paused to have a sip of beer, as though the words tasted bad in his mouth and he was anxious to be rid of them.

'Cooper's Cove is a series of caves on the shoreline,' Rob said to Dean. 'You can only access it at low tide. Once the tide comes back in you're totally fucked.'

'What was it you think you saw?' Dean asked Paul.

'A flash of bright green,' Paul said. 'And Susan was reported as having a lime green cagoule, right?'

'Yeah,' muttered Rob. 'That's what the police said.'

'The police are usually pretty thorough, though,' Dean offered. 'How come they didn't check out the cove as part of their investigation?'

'Cooper's Cove is not a cakewalk,' Rob interjected. 'The local council sealed it in the seventies after three tourists got caught by the tide and drowned. This place is dead enough even with punters coming here during the summer.'

'So the police didn't inspect Cooper's Cove because they thought it was inaccessible?' Dean concluded.

'Partly,' Rob said. 'But there was the copper's assurance he saw Susan at the opposite end of town. They had no need to consider the cove.'

That makes some sense.

'Maybe I should've said something,' Paul said as he stared into his glass. 'Life sucks, doesn't it?'

'You can't be sure that you saw anything,' Rob said. 'That storm was a force six. It could have been a trick of the light, the fucking waves dragging in a buoy, anything.'

Paul nodded, but the gesture lacked gusto and his eyes held doubt. The youth's life was mire and he was barely keeping his head in the open air. He'd eventually convinced himself that he had seen nothing. In Dean's mind, the chances that Paul had witnessed a glimpse of Susan Hadley that day were growing. The barriers were rising on an unexplored avenue.

However, Dean understood Paul's dilemma. Based on police statistics, kids in care had a propensity to come into contact with the criminal justice system more often than not. Paul didn't want to test those odds by reporting what he'd seen and ending up a suspect if thoughts turned from a simple accident to foul play. Instead, he had kept quiet, and uncertainty created a solid rationale to remain that way.

'What about the girl's parents?' Dean asked. 'Do they still live locally?'

'So where do you come from, mister?' Paul replied.

Dean pulled a confused face. The two youths were staring at him dolefully as though he'd not asked his question.

'I come from Birmingham,' he said quickly. 'Now what about Mr and Mrs Hadley? It must've been awful for them.'

'I've never been out of Gullcrest,' Rob said. The kid's eyes seemed vague and his tone of voice was lilting, as though he was about to start singing. Instead, the youth began to whistle. It was a tune Dean recognised but couldn't quite place, but rather than bring relief to the event, the refrain merely added another bizarre layer to proceedings. Coupled with this, Paul was sitting beside him smiling as though a good memory had come to mind.

A shadow fell across their table, taking the focus away from their discussion. Dean turned to see Grimes standing over them. He had his arms crossed against his barrelled chest, and his face was deadpan.

'Think you lads have had enough,' he said to Rob and Paul.

'You're kidding, right?' Rob said with an uncertain grin. He was back in the room, all traces of vagueness gone.

The expression on the publican's face told them he wasn't kidding at all.

'If you lads leave now then, perhaps, I won't have to rethink whether letting you come in here is a good idea or not,' Grimes said.

Dean saw it for what it was, a warning that the conversation was over. Rob and Paul didn't need telling twice. They quickly finished their drinks and left without giving Dean more than a courteous glance.

Grimes remained where he was and his gaze fell upon Dean. 'Kids these days, eh? They just open their mouths and shit pours out.' His voice carried about as much warmth as it did truth.

Dean wasn't as convinced. 'They seemed pretty sober to me.'

'What? You mean like you are, sir?' Grimes said.

That hit home. Dean wanted to reply but held himself in check. Cages had been rattled this evening and he wasn't about to create more trouble by breaking the lock and having to deal with the beast he'd let loose.

'I guess I'd better get myself off to bed,' he said, moving away from the table.

'I guess you had,' Grimes said. 'And this bar is out of bounds to you from this point on, sir.'

'Why?'

'We both know why,' Grimes said. 'The press is not welcome in my bar. I've made that mistake before.'

Dean didn't protest. There were plenty of places where he could get his poison. Besides, what he'd gleaned tonight had him fuelled in ways not even booze could compete.

Far from being a dead end, the story of Susan Hadley's disappearance was coming back to life like Frankenstein's monster.

* * *

Dean didn't have to be a journalist to know that news travelled fast. This wasn't any less true than small communities. By the time he went down to the reception area the next morning, he sensed the atmosphere was different. Gone was the tranquil air. It was replaced instead by a taut tension that seemed almost palpable. As he passed by the Chesterfield sofas, the elderly couple from the bar gave him a glance and pretended to scrutinise their guide books.

As he approached the reception counter, Dean found the stare emanating from Defu was relentless. The receptionist's lips were pursed in disdain as contempt made itself comfortable.

'Morning,' he said regardless. 'Any messages before I head into town?'

'Out to dig up more dirt, are we?' Defu said coldly. 'A writer, you said. Tsk, you should be ashamed.'

'Well, I'm not,' Dean said with a smile.

'I'm not surprised,' she sneered. 'Your type has no shame. You don't care about how such a thing can affect a community.'

'What about how such a thing affects the parents?' Dean contested.
'No one has heard their side of things. Maybe talking to me, sharing their terrible experience, is a way to help them move on? It may even help others who have lost loved ones.'

The lilting tune he'd heard on Rob's and Paul's lips was back in the air. He recognised it as the children's nursery rhyme, "Ten Green Bottles", yet the tune was eerie and maudlin, as though sung as a funeral dirge.

Dean turned to search for its source but, other than the couple on the sofas, the reception area was devoid of other people. Then his ears located its origin.

Defu was humming the tune as she absently filled in a booking form on the counter. She wasn't looking at him anymore; all contempt had fallen away from her. It was as though he simply didn't exist to her. He placed his key card on the desk and left the hotel, intrigued as well as bemused.

On his way to the car, Dean considered the events of the past twenty-four hours. Not only had Cound's suspicions of a story been confirmed, it was shaping into something neither of them had envisaged. He fought to keep his heart steady. Sure, he had expected the aloof behaviours exhibited by the locals towards him once they'd realised he was a journalist. Hell, he was used to it.

But this was something different, something off-kilter. If he was honest, he was feeling pretty freaked out. Yet such a nuance didn't have him pointing the MR2 inland and back to the city. Instead, it energised his desire to find out what the fuck was going on.

He pulled the car out onto the narrow track that snaked the small coastal road where Gullcrest nestled in an enclave two miles away.

The ocean lay to his left and, under the morning sun, the expanse of water was a shimmering entity that the relentless breeze caressed. The waves sent sea spray onto the window screen where it was wiped away by intermittent wiper blades.

Dean was having more of an issue when it came to clearing his mind. As well as the events of that morning, he was still having trouble with the dream. It didn't help since the images had no chronology and left a disjointed and shocking array of brutal images. Then there was the girl, Susan Hadley, being dragged away from her home on a stormy night.

There was no getting away from just how unsettled he felt by recent developments. Well, there was one way; a few days in the company of Ol' Jim would do it. But he was reluctant. Where there was a story, Ol' Jim took a back seat; that was always the deal. His addiction didn't melt away, it was just reshaped, the thrill of chasing down a scoop replacing the desire for oblivion in amber liquor. And as far as the story went, part of him was not only digging in, it was preparing to bring out the heavy plant machinery and go burrowing beneath the surface to see what was hiding there.

No matter how dark things turned out.

* * *

The low ceilings and tall, free-standing book cases gave Gullcrest library an oppressive atmosphere. There were three small windows through which the sun tried hard to make its presence felt, but the book cases in certain sections cast dour grey shadows on those milling through the aisles.

Dean had found a small reading table at the far end of the square room. The librarian, a tall slim man with black, greasy hair and a pencil-thin moustache, fussed over the returns pile. Every so often the librarian would cast a suspicious glance in his direction, a process that started as soon as Dean had walked in and had asked if it was okay for him to browse.

In reality, Dean didn't want to wade through reference books; he wanted solitude and access to Wi-Fi not on offer at the Olde Majestic Hotel. He spent three hours surfing the web to try to establish more information on Susan's disappearance, but all roads on the information super highway just led him into the undergrowth.

Local news reports were simply an exercise in journalism by numbers, facile narratives with little substance. His frustration allowed a craving for Ol' Jim to surface shortly before the conversation with Rob and Paul came back to him, slapping it away. The recollection focused on Paul's admission that he'd witnessed something down on the beach, near the place he'd referred to as Cooper's Cove.

Dean punched the name into the search browser and scanned the data that came up on the screen. After alighting on a few websites, he settled for one that gave Cooper's Cove some history and sent this to the printer sitting behind the librarian's counter. Dean packed up his laptop, stowing it inside a brown leather satchel, and headed for the printer, fishing out his wallet in preparation to pay the printout fee.

The librarian turned to the staccato sound of the Xerox next to him. When the feed had finished, he retrieved the sheets of paper from the tray with fingers that were long and delicate.

'How much do I owe you?' Dean asked in a hushed voice. Libraries had a way of robbing his voice, a throw back from school, and the memories of the dragon of a librarian he'd encountered on one too many occasions.

'More than you can repay.' The librarian's voice came not as a whisper but as a contemptuous hiss.

Dean understood the jibe immediately. He looked at the name tag on the lapel of the man's tweed waistcoat. It told him the librarian had been christened Jonathan Horton. 'Look, I don't want any trouble,' he offered. 'I'm just doing some research.'

'What's next?' Horton said. 'Taking a spade up to her memorial and digging up the only thing they could bury? A teddy bear she'd had from birth. You people make me sick.'

Horton prepared to tear the sheets of paper. The librarian did it deliberately, his brown eyes staring at Dean as though gauging, revelling, in his response.

Dean's first thought was to grab Horton's thin wrists and drag him over the counter. He composed himself. Being arrested for assault and the theft of several sheets of paper was not on the agenda today. Just when he felt that his sharp mind was going to dump him on his arse, Dean had an epiphany. As soon as realisation came to him, it steamrolled and filled in a few blanks.

'You said "they",' Dean said to Horton.

The librarian stopped. The sheets - held horizontally at chest height and ready to be torn in half - trembled in his hands.

'What?'

'You said "they",' Dean repeated. 'Not *Susan's parents*, but "they". Is there a problem acknowledging the girl's parents in this town?'

Horton's eyes adopted the vacant, serene glaze that was fast becoming familiar to Dean.

The librarian let go of the sheets of paper and they drifted lazily onto the counter where they scattered. The mesmerised man reached into his pocket and withdrew a mobile phone that he placed before him.

Dean watched in fascination as the twig-thin fingers, that only moments before were about to tear his printouts to shreds, massaged the keypad on the mobile and generated a series of tones.

It should have left Dean dumbstruck but the resulting tune in the air only confirmed what he already knew. He scooped up the papers and left a five pound note on the counter. Throughout this, Horton continued his ritual on the key pad.

Dean left the library, racing down the steps, and allowed its heavy doors to close, cutting off the electronic beeps from Horton's mobile phone.

Even as he put distance between himself and Gullcrest's librarian, the bright discordant rendition of "Ten Green Bottles" still bounced around Dean's brain as though presenting the perfect soundtrack to the pervading sense of madness.

* * *

The gulls wheeled overhead and only the intermittent crashing of waves against rocks blocked out their incessant screeches. Just like the rest of the inhabitants of Gullcrest, the birds weren't used to intruders in their domain.

At least inhospitality is a constant, Dean thought as he clambered up to the cove.

His clothes were damp from sea spray and his shoes were full of sand. It didn't help to improve his intense dislike for the beach. He'd had such an aversion to the seaside for as long as he could remember, though he did not recall a catalyst for it. He couldn't even blame it on Jenna. If anyone asked him why he avoided such places, he would have told them that he just felt dirty after spending more than a few minutes in the company of coarse sand, shale, and the sea with its high silage content.

Using the map he'd printed off at the library, he'd traipsed across the sand to get to Cooper's Cove, cursing every single step as the fine grains found every access point in his loafers. His only other companion was a small Magna-lite he'd dragged from the glove box. Finding Cooper's Cove was easy enough—a set of stone steps, green with moss and slimy seaweed, led from the promenade to the beach. From there it was a half-mile walk, the sand making it feel a lot further.

Accessing the cove wasn't straightforward either. The council had placed a barrier of webbed orange plastic sheeting across the path in the rocks, and Dean had to traverse left and scramble over three huge, limpet-encrusted boulders that scraped the skin off of his hands and shins. He allowed his curses to keep him company and had pretty much exhausted his vocabulary of expletives by the time he'd circumvented the barrier and rejoined the path.

Sodden and out of breath, he went over the place's potted history in a bid to keep him focused.

The cove took its name from a local fisherman, James Cooper, who was awarded the honour having discovered a pirate's hoard back in the seventeen hundreds. According to the literature, the unfortunate Cooper was later found face down in the ocean. When pulled free from the water by the locals, his bloated body had the Ace of Spades rammed into his mouth; the mark of a pirate traitor. Under suspicions, Cooper knew of the pirate booty in the cove because he was also involved in putting it there, the local village council removed the accolade. Instead, his body was hung in the mouth of the cave and left for the gulls.

Yet from this point on, with or without official sanction, the area would forever be known as Cooper's Cove. Local folklore had it that on the first full moon of each month, Cooper's spectre haunted the cove that had cursed his final days.

Under normal circumstances, Dean would have enjoyed reading more about the superstitions based around the area. But this was a luxury he just could not afford. The routes in the Susan Hadley case were leading him to this spot. And nothing could distract him from his course.

Despite this, he noted with some frustration, that up ahead the mouth of the cave was firmly closed. Sheets of corrugated metal had been riveted together and placed across the entrance. Here they were secured to the rock face with huge bolts that were rusted with age and the daily abuse from the ocean. Where the sea had beaten against the barrier during high tide, the metal surface was splashed with greens and browns. But it still appeared steadfast, with no obvious way for Dean to go any farther.

He walked along the outcrop; the waves pummelled the hem of the rocks some twenty feet below. The metal sheets began to tower over him until he felt like Tolkien's grey wizard standing at the gates of Moria. He placed his hands against the barrier and the cold metal was shocking on the skin of his palms.

Dead end. He peered along the rock face either side of the sealed entrance. Instinct told him there was something more. There always was, after all. Such a conclusion was supported by the Hadley story. A little more probing and there it had been, a cold trail now warm once more; a beacon to light the way towards a Pulitzer.

Then there's the dream.

The thought was there before he could head it off. He needn't have worried; he saw something in the rock face before he had the chance to become absorbed by the images haunting his consciousness.

Several feet to the right of the cave entrance, something caught his attention in the gnarled, gull-shit splattered rocks. It was an indent, a dark crevice that to the naked eye shouldn't have aroused any suspicion at all.

For Dean, suspicion had become innate. It came as part of having a sister who was forever trying to get the jump on him. The indent, a horizontal groove—three inches long and two deep— was too regular, too uniform to be made by nature. Man had a hand in its inception and, no sooner had such a thought scuttled into his mind, he instinctively reached out to it and used it as doctrine.

He slid his fingers into the slot where he found a small lever that succumbed easily to his touch, creating a small buzzing sound. Part of the rock face near to the metal sheets appeared to recede for a few feet, allowing room for someone to bypass the barrier with ease.

Sly door, he thought, but the grin on his lips betrayed his delight. Secret doors existed only to keep secrets. And secrets meant stories and roads to glory.

On the threshold of his discovery, he took a breath and savoured the moment. The waves below crashed into the rocks; his heart beat out its rhythm against his chest.

Dean fired up the Magna-lite and, as the gulls screamed as though citing his actions as folly, he stepped inside.

* * *

The torch did its best but the darkness beyond was consuming. The beam threw down a milky pool that appeared suffocated by the inky blackness. In this meagre half-light Dean could make out huge rocks, rounded by the ocean's relentless caress.

Even with the ironclad Canute blocking the entrance the mighty ocean showed evidence that it could never be repelled. As Dean moved deeper into the cave, seawater washed against his shoes as he stepped into large puddles and, within moments, his socks were saturated. Huge droplets fell from the ceiling high above and, after a haphazard journey of several hundred feet, laid flat Dean's hair with the ceaseless downpour.

The dark and the wet were an irrelevance to him. The story was all and, with every passing second, it called to him like a siren's song luring a hapless sailor towards the waiting, jagged rocks. He moved deeper into this netherworld, his footfalls morphing into eerie, elongated growls, the torch beam flitting across the undulating walls in fleeting bursts of brilliance.

The cave appeared to go on forever. Dean had been walking for what felt like ages when he realised the darkness was losing its density. He was able to see beyond the beam and, just as he contemplated the source, a sudden flicker-flash of light almost made him cry out in surprise.

Initially blinded by the flare of lights, he covered his eyes with his hands; the Magna-lite fell to the ground where a puddle snuffed out its bulb. He used his fingers to shield his eyes as they adjusted to the wall lights; huge things of thick, rounded glass and caged behind heavy-duty mesh. The lights were embedded into a wall made of smooth grey concrete.

'What the fuck?'

This statement was not aimed at the unexpected brilliance about him. It was an acknowledgement that the cave had come to an abrupt end.

And at the centre of this wall, was a door.

* * *

The door was made of bright, shimmering steel and, while it sparkled under the touch of the halogen lamps, the mysterious gateway was featureless. To its left, halfway and sunken into the concrete, was a square, white key pad.

Fascinated, Dean approached the panel and examined the digits imbued into its surface. It was a standard security access device, with a small, rectangular display window fitted horizontally at its apex and key pads beneath. He leaned forward to see if any keys were worn with overuse, an old trick a private investigator had taught him on one of Dean's many early assignments.

There were no telltale scuffs or marks. Dean took this as a sign that codes were frequently changed. This made him stall for a moment. If codes were frequently changed, then perhaps this indicated the door was still being used.

It still held its secrets.

His heart scudding, Dean reached for the panel and his finger hovered over its surface. His hesitation wasn't about what might be lurking beyond the steel door, though this wasn't far from his mind, but bemusement as to how he could possibly bypass the random security code.

But you do know the code, don't you, Deano? Jenna was in his head, caustic and brash. *She showed you, remember? The little girl in your dream. She showed you.*

Eight, eight, one, eight.

Slowly his fingers played on the panel. He didn't think about it, he just recalled the dream—the rain and the screams and a small slip of paper falling at his feet to reveal a number opening a door in a subterranean lair.

He mouthed the digits as he typed them, cursing a few times as his trembling fingers hit the wrong buttons twice, requiring him to hit the cancel key. A small bleep, made bigger by the cave, announced that his efforts had been successful. This was followed by a dull, heavy thud as the tumblers disengaged and the door eased slowly open with a protracted hum.

Dean peered into the opening, trepidation making movement hesitant. A short corridor lay ahead, lit by stark fluorescents. Something else kept him standing in the doorway. The air smelled bad, a fundamental foetid stink that had his stomach rolling. He covered his mouth with a hand, the thumb and index finger squeezing his nostrils closed and he breathed through pursed lips.

The corridor opened out at the far end. Even from a distance of twenty feet, he could see the surgical tables and cabinets of a laboratory. And, even more unsettling, the tables were occupied.

Again, intrigue overcame fear and Dean crept down the corridor until he was able to see the entire lab.

It was a huge room, easily forty feet square, and filled with a dizzying array of sights, a sensory overload of horror that, for a moment, had him bringing up his other hand to plug the vomit threatening to rise from his belly.

He closed his eyes to give his mind time to adjust, but the images were branded into his brain.

Three of the walls comprised holding pens, and the glass doors were daubed with red and brown streaks. Beyond this vivid curtain, things moved and he had difficulty making them out. Deep down he knew what he'd seen inside the pens could not be catagorised, since fringe science had been playing merrily down here in the bowels of the earth.

This was borne out by the lab tables standing between him and the holding pens - several of them; each occupied with things that had started out as human beings. Yet what was left was difficult to fathom.

He could see naked torsos and limbs, the flesh about them ruddy and sporting livid scratches and surgical slashes. Abdomens had been opened out so that the world could look in; the skin peeled back and held in place by a haphazard line of fat staples which puckered the fat and muscle. Stomach cavities disgorged thick, black pipes that ran into five demijohns, each filled with a green, viscous fluid.

Each table played host to similar atrocities, all with their innards being fed by piping and racks of bottles, and this was not the only thing they had in common. Mercifully every cadaver had its face covered with a white sheet. Dean's macabre sense of curiosity pulled him closer. He focused on the flimsy cloth covering the head of the occupant of the nearest table, his feet squeaking on the linoleum. He fought to ignore the gaping hole in the chest to his left, and the pipes spilling from it. With a trembling hand he lifting the sheet, and peered underneath.

'Jesus fucking Christ!'

He staggered away from the table, backing into a trolley that clanged noisily against the wall. Dean's hand remained enmeshed in the sheet and dragged it with him and he inadvertently unveiled the monstrosity to the room.

There was a head; there was a face, but it didn't belong. It didn't fit in the way nature intended. In fact, what had been exposed was an assault on convention, Mother Nature dragged into the darkness and raped, a dirty hand clamped over her mouth.

It was a human torso, a human neck, but beyond that, the head belonged to a wolf. Its mouth was pulled back into a leer, and a long, pink tongue lolled onto the plinth supporting its muzzle. There was a hyphened line of sutures at the stump of a dirty brown neck, attaching beast to man. Yet Dean was both reviled and fascinated. When the creature's eyes fluttered open a weak, pathetic whimper emerged from the muzzle, Dean thought sanity had decided to go on a field trip.

The bastard creation of science was alive!

It was weak and incapacitated, but it lived as any other creature. He sought purchase on the trolley behind him, and his splayed fingers caught something heavy.

He tore his gaze away from the incredible sight languishing on the table and saw a bulky and battered leather-bound book. There was no lettering on its cover, just a crisscross of creases.

He lifted the book, the leather greasy under his touch, and a sharp, pungent odour rose from the cover, wrinkling his nostrils. He flipped open the pages. Dean scanned a variety of meticulous, detailed drawings furnished in both pencil and ink. Many of them were anatomical diagrams of the creatures about him; others were cross sections of cells and tissue. All of them were accompanied by a fine, flowing script. The pages were a work of art but of a terrible sort, the kind that belied the blurring of madness and genius. And when Dean rifled through the journal and found the signature on the first page, this gained even greater clarity.

Professor Jonathan Green.

'Well, well,' Dean mused, the awful sights now forgotten as the journalist inside him called up for duty. 'You old bastard,' he whispered. 'So this is where you've been hiding? This is what you've been doing.'

Green was as brilliant as he was controversial, always the prey for eager newshounds who craved an interview with the nefarious professor. Green had breezed through Oxford with first class and masters' degrees in molecular and cellular biochemistry and pure chemistry, a natural flair for science carving him a niche in the field of biomedical research.

An accomplished geneticist, Green had input into several high-profile scientific breakthroughs, but there were rumours from his critics that his results were so innovative, not all of his studies could possibly be ethically sound. Indeed, by the time the Medical Research Council wanted to discuss unauthorised clinical trials on human subjects, Green fell off of the radar and hadn't been seen in more than five years.

Dean had covered the story of Green's disappearance, but had pretty much concluded the professor was on the run, using his ample financial resources to remain hidden.

The laboratory suggested Green's wealth had been used to other ends, a means to continue his work, his religion, and he'd built himself a ghastly altar at which he could worship. Dean was under no illusion that the journal he currently held in his trembling hands was not so much a bible, but a grimoire from which Green's alchemy spewed out into the scientific world. The professor had become a god, creating creatures that were not meant to exist, crafting them like a deranged toymaker in a quest for—

Dean stopped.

A quest for what? Such vile things done in the name of science, but it had to have some purpose, right? Or was Green truly insane and somewhere among the monstrosities, behind glass and the body parts on surgical tables, were the piteous remnants of a little girl who had ventured where she shouldn't have?

Dean scanned the text, his eyes alighting on certain paragraphs, taking them in before moving on. Some of the script was so laden with scientific jargon, his brain struggled to comprehend. Occasionally sentences rose to the surface of this literary Sargasso. But it was a chunk of letters ring-fenced by an untidy oval of red ink that snared his attention.

'The regenerative enzyme P138 is a success! The results from Subject 37 conclude substantive moderation of the Lamin A protein. Progeria, this accursed disease, is in its final moments. Soon I must turn my intentions to the scientific casualties about me. It is a necessary evil in order to expound the boundaries of knowledge. People may not understand my methods but perhaps, in time, they may understand my motives. What father would not?'

Beneath the text was a series of deftly drawn pictures which showed images of people who appeared slight and frail, their heads disproportionately large and hairless; eyes appeared as though they would pop from their sockets at any given moment. Dean presumed that what he was seeing was the effects of the very illness Green intended to conquer. The questions were: why and at what cost?

Dean had no opportunity to linger on his queries. An unexpected sound interrupted him. The hiss and creak of a door sliding open. Dean turned to see a figure emerge from a vestibule at the other side of the room. It was wearing a white biochemical suit and a bulky mask with twin canisters either side of a rubber-coated chin. Dean made to run back to the exit, but he saw the silver object the figure held in its hand shortly before the "phut!" as the air-driven gun spat something across the room and into his abdomen.

A sudden, stinging sensation took hold of his midriff followed by a total collapse of his muscles. From far away he heard himself say 'fuck', but in reality it came out as a thin stream of saliva as his lips lost control and the sudden warmth of urine as it coursed down his jeans.

He staggered, legs jelly, arms leaden. As he fell, bouncing off of a lab table, he recognised that bottles were racked on both sides of each table. Five of them. Ten in total. All filled with green fluid that was being fed into the organs of the things beneath the sheets.

Ten green bottles, in fact.

As the tune rattled about his head, Dean's frozen lips tried to smile.

Then came the voice, small and fragile in the huge rushing din in his head, as blood pumped through dilated capillaries. A child's voice, a girl's, and she was calling to him to find her. To save her.

Even as he tried to focus, his eyes blurred, the lab becoming nothing more than an unstable image of shimmering ripples. He wanted to call out, tell the girl he was looking for her, that he'd tracked her all the way to this place - this hell - and he didn't want to give up on her like so many others seemingly had.

But the drugs pumping through his veins turned thought to stupor and, by the time unconsciousness consumed him, Dean could no longer hear the girl's pleas over the sounds of his own fervent screams.

VIRUS UNLEASHED!

A huge, searing pain brought Dean back to consciousness. It pierced his brain, bringing with it a wave of nausea that had him rolling onto his side when he retched several times but produced nothing more than wads of thick phlegm. He flopped onto his back and draped his forearm across his eyes in an attempt to shut out the stark, relentless lights feeding his headache. His breathing was heavy and he used its rhythm as a means to focus his mind away from his affliction. The pain was slowly retreating and in the wasteland it left behind, the events of the past few days took a chance and began to advance.

Disjointed images flitted into his head like a poorly edited movie, but it still made a surreal kind of sense. When Dean recalled the professor's ledger, realisation purged the last vestiges of the tranquiliser and its effects.

'Fucker shot me,' he mumbled. He risked sitting up, the process tentative for fear of antagonising his shuddering skull. He looked about him, and the lab was gone. Instead, he was in a cubical, the walls white and smooth save for one made from a slab of thick glass.

It was a cell, one of those he'd seen upon entering the lab. Dean made for the transparent barrier, his heart thumping as he tried to suffocate the notion he was locked in forever. However, as he got closer, a small, vertical gap could be seen to his left where the glass cell door was not quite in contact with the frame. He reached out for the edge, the breeze coming through the space bringing with it the smell of the ocean. It was welcomed; a small piece of normality invading the reek of lab chemicals and urine from his soiled pants.

He paused as his fingertips hooked into the few centimetres the gap allowed. He pulled, half expecting the door to not move at all. To his relief, the glass pane slid smoothly for a few centimetres before it abruptly stopped.

But no obstacle barred its progress. Dean had paused in order to check the scene beyond. In his haste to be free, he'd almost forgotten the circumstances. He peered through the glass. The lab was in disarray. Tables had been overturned, the bottles smashed and their contents spilled onto the tiles as sickly green puddles. There was no sign of the things that had been lying on the tables, just crumpled sheets stained with brown and green goo. He considered whether the journal remained somewhere in the lab, evidence he could take with him in order to expose Green's ghastly deeds to a vengeful public. Dean knew to search for it would be pointless. The dart that had put him out for a while was a thing of purpose, a cloak to aid the perpetuation of deadly deceit. There would be no journal, there couldn't be.

The lab was deserted, and the need to leave his cage overwhelmed him. He continued to slide the glass door aside until he'd created enough space to squeeze through. It was tight but a precaution just in case the lab held any more surprises for him, the kind that moved and snarled when they shouldn't exist at all. Should such an event take place, his cell would have to become his refuge for a while.

Be prepared. His brief stint in the Scouting Association at the tender age of eleven hadn't been a total waste of time after all. He smiled at the thought, but his eyes remained bright with anxiety as he stepped free and made his way through the lab.

Thousands of glittering, tiny cubes were strewn across the floor, mixed with the spillage from the demijohns. Dean looked at the other cells, where the glass partitions had been obliterated. Then he drew in air and held it as he realised the implications.

The stalls were empty. The creatures were loose!

He heard the growl seconds before the lights went out. The darkness was total, a suffocating, ebony cloak that had him releasing a sharp cry that he aborted with a hand as he slapped it against his mouth with such force his lips mashed into his teeth, drawing blood.

His breath came as tiny shuddering gasps as he listened. He'd heard something before the dark came. A small sound, a sound animalistic in quality. A growl? No, not a growl, something more sinister.

A snarl. Feral and determined.

The darkness had brought something with it, something that was snuffling and snorting in a bid to seek him out.

He remained stock still, though fear was playing with his muscles of his legs, making them do small jittery dances. Not all of the beasts had left the lab, it seemed.

At least he now had the inky blackness about him as an ally. He was just asking himself how long he could hold out when, just as suddenly as they'd failed; the lights came back on, momentarily dazzling him.

The snarl became a hideous prolonged howl and, through the halogen haze, Dean made out a large humanoid shape charging towards him, knocking aside clinical debris as though it had no substance at all.

Just as instinct drove the creature, Dean's own nuances of self-preservation had him turning and charging headlong, away from the lab—from the beast—in the direction of the exit. Part of him screamed a warning; what if the escapee experiments were waiting for him in the cave, eager to get their claws and teeth into his flesh?

But while this was not sure-fire, the thing chasing him down certainly was; its guttural barks came like a portent of his fate should he not get the hell out of there.

His feet slithered in a pool of goo and the heel of his shoe drew a shitty zigzag on the tiles before he managed to straighten himself. His side caught against an upended table, his hip taking a blow and sending a sharp jolt of pain through his pelvis. He cried out but kept moving, the desire to avoid the thing slavering behind him overriding his discomfort.

The exit drew tantalisingly close, a rectangular gateway that heralded sanctuary—sanity—from a world gone mad. But, at that moment, madness was alive and well in the thing sending huge blasts of foetid air onto his neck and shoulders. He cried out again. This time in desperation, he could see himself being grabbed and shredded only inches from refuge. He managed to gain more strength, the muscles of his legs burning like brands against his skin, adrenaline dulling his hip to a white heat.

Three feet and he would be through.

Two feet and the creature's breath came as a vile spray on the back of his neck.

Dean dived—outstretched and headlong—for the gap in the door. He got through, but the exit was untidy. His shoulder took some of the impact, sending him left where he rolled onto his back and the unforgiving rocks on the cave floor punished his body.

Adrenaline—and the desire to live—had him moving immediately. The thing that had chased him down had hit the door seconds later and ploughed through, its impressive size swinging the metal slab wide, and momentum carrying it into the cave in a flurry of snarls and writhing water.

The beast rose from the cave pool, its height and bulk leaving Dean agog. The halogens played upon its putrid pink-and-purple hide, the dermis stripped away and pulsating veins and capillaries which crisscrossed the skin like the frenzied scribbles of a deranged child. It stood at least seven feet tall, each gangling limb fusing rigid muscle with sinister elegance. The face was nothing more than an angled network of bone, a skull slapped on top of foetid flesh. This was man's ultimate affront to God, an organic machine bent on slaughter. Dean saw no conscience or sense of morality in the bulbous, black eyes staring at him, nor did he see any other expression in a cavernous mouth bristling with vicious, misshapen teeth and dripping thick saliva like a cataract viewed in slow motion. He saw only the wanton lust of a starving animal, hairless and horrific, and ready to charge him down.

Dean had only one chance as the beast gained its bearings. What was clear to him was that this thing was fuelled by a base desire to feed; its frenzied actions suggested it was almost insane with the desire of it, and Dean was the preferred morsel of choice. Where he went, the creature was sure to follow with the same unfettered, salivating fervour. He had to use this tenet and fast.

Dean scuttled to his knees, the pain in his shoulder and hip numbed by fear. As he stood, bowed with fatigue and gasping for air, the creature's bald, ballooned head turned and fixed on him.

It moved, faster than he would have thought possible given its bulk. Yet Dean was ready. As the beast lunged for him, mouth agape and grey tongue lolling, Dean threw himself sideways. In its haste to get hold of him, the creature continued its charge and crashed into the corridor. Massive thuds and crashes resounded as its huge shape met concrete floor and walls.

He clambered to his feet and smashed a palm against the access panel in the wall. The door sighed as it began to close but the sound was stifled by a series of familiar angry barks from the corridor beyond. Then came the thin, scraping din of claws as they tried to take purchase on concrete. He leapt back as the snarls came at him through a sliver of space, shortly before the hydraulics kicked in and powered the door shut. The frustrated cries were silenced as comprehensively as an off switch silenced a radio. Now the only sound was the small whimpers as Dean wept with relief.

Several heavy thuds hit the door, startling him. The beast was not quite ready to quit, it seemed. Dean made his way back through the cave, the rectangular entrance framed by daylight seeping in through the metal, a faraway beacon in the terrible darkness.

Slowly, deliberately, he made his way towards it.

* * *

The first thing that hit him was the acrid reek of burning materials. He emerged from the cave and the sea breeze brought the stink to him, making him blink as the sting of smoke and the dazzling daylight battled to lay bare his senses. He paused in an attempt to find his bearings. As his eyes adjusted he could see Gullcrest in the distance and realised his victory in Green's laboratory was token.

The town was a writhing mass of flame and destruction. From his elevated position in the rocks, Dean could see fire already had several buildings in its grip and, even as he watched, a huge explosion punched skywards, scattering flaps of black material into the air. The sheeting appeared to hang in the sky for a time, like twisted kites on a deadly breeze, before plummeting back down to earth with heavy, distant slaps as they hit the concrete streets.

The horror that was occurring in those streets had Dean recalling his awful dream from the previous night; the brutality was the catalyst but there was a difference from the dreadful images from his dream, the nightmare made real as it played out before him.

The cobblestone streets of Gullcrest were teeming with activity. People and the creatures from Green's lab were welded together in an undulating mass of blood and flesh. Dean fought to stay objective, even though madness was pacing the fringes of conscious thought.

It's all about the story, Deano. You've got to keep it together. You've got to let people know what the hell is going on!

There were more creatures than Dean had seen in Green's cells back at the lab. And he began questioning how a handful of experimental throwbacks could become an army of tearing, ripping monsters, too many to count.

And now this vile army was venting its wrath on the townsfolk, hauling limbs from their sockets, discarding them as if they had no value in the feeding frenzy. Gouts of blood would spray in arcs and the thin, terrible screams of the mutilated drifted across the beach.

Dean's knees wanted to give out but he widened his stance just to add balance. Instinct had him wanting to turn tail and head back into the cave, but reason turned up to the gig and he peered down at the rising tide. In a few hours he'd be cut off and the only peace he would find would be eternal, instigated by lungs bloated with sea water.

He had no choice. It was both drown and let the story die with him. Or get to his car and out of town to the hotel, where he could contact Cound and begin the process of telling the world of current events at Gullcrest. It would be an exclusive, an up-close-and-personal account by the only reporter on the scene at the time. It was Pulitzer stuff; it was what he'd always dreamed.

No contest, no choice.

With a huge sigh, Dean made his way down towards the beach and headed cautiously towards Hell.

* * *

The screams were both ear-splitting and heart-rending. As Dean made his way across the beach, he hunkered as low as his aching hip and shoulder would allow. He turned sharply at a sudden explosion of sand to his left and he looked at the object that had landed there.

It was a small hatchet, blade splashed with the same green liquid he'd seen in the bottles. The hatchet didn't come alone; a hand—large and severed at the elbow—gripped onto the wooden stave, the fingers blanched and a wedding band glinting in the mid-afternoon sun.

He managed to see beyond the grisly item cast down onto the sand like driftwood abandoned by the tide. He scuttled over to the limb and gently pried the fingers away from the hatchet. His face twisted with disgust as each digit emitted a pop or a crack under the pressure.

Dean looked down at the paltry implement, and wondered just how effective it would be against Green's brood. He closed his mind to the idea that its previous owner had perhaps found out, literally, first-hand. Still, the weight of the hatchet gave him some sense of security; irrespective of how misguided such a notion may yet prove.

Ahead, weathered stone steps led to the promenade. The high wall of huge, roughly hewn chunks of grey-green stone was crowned with black railings. As he peered upwards, Dean could see limbs poking through the horizontal strips of wrought iron. Blood cascaded from the summit in thick, ugly streams of deep crimson that splattered onto the sand as dirty brown smudges.

The steps were the only way off of the beach and Dean's reluctance to climb them, to rise from the relative safety the sand afforded into the chaos and carnage above, manifested as his legs shivered in fear.

Fuckin' move, Deano, Jenna chastised in his head. *You want that story or not? Or maybe you want to sit on the beach like some landlocked hermit and kid yourself that those things ain't going to come for you when the food runs out.*

The food? People?

Jenna the mercenary was already rationalising his options.

While Green's lab rats are chowing down on the townsfolk, maybe they'll be distracted enough for you to slip through unnoticed. More chance now than later when the meat is all gone, right?

He heaved at the thought of innocent people being labelled as nothing more than foodstuff for the monstrosities running riot above. Already the screams were thinning out. Mankind was losing the battle. Dean had to move now, before it was too late, and he was spotted as soon as he got onto the promenade.

He dragged himself onwards, his ascent shuddering as the horizontal summit neared and the violence became a palpable commodity. As he peeked over the top of the wall nothing, not even the dream, could have prepared him for the scene that met him.

The streets were a twisted, tangled forest of human remains, severed limbs rising from foliage of mauled meat. Those people, who still fought, skittered on cobblestones slick with blood as they tried to push back against the fury the creatures brought with them.

As Dean watched, a man in the rags of a police uniform held up a pistol and pumped three bullets into a beast that ran at him. Two rounds punched into the creature's abdomen, their impact marked by tiny violet plumes, but the onwards momentum was not swayed until the third bullet blew open its head. Like a puppet with strings suddenly severed, the creature collapsed and skidded to a halt at the police officer's shoes. To Dean the sight was almost symbolic; man was still king of the world despite the horrors placed upon it. And this police officer—this last bastion of law enforcement and order—was a beacon of hope in the coming darkness. Behind such thoughts, Dean could see his news piece unfolding before him on the screen of his laptop. And just as the stoic act of shooting the beast had elevated the police officer to iconic status, so words would take Dean to equal standing as a window on the world for this brief and terrible time.

The gun spoke again; another creature was sent crashing through the plate glass window of a grocer's shop. Vegetables and fruit tumbled from their display stands, all coated with green and purple slime. Dean moved towards the police officer, as did the other people who were still not either maimed or paralysed by fear, a ragtag and terrified ensemble that, like Dean, saw the officer as their champion.

This perspective was enhanced by the creatures' reaction. They had amassed at one end of the street, cautious and still. Dean saw the reticence in their gait, fury held in check by the need to survive. They had lost two of their number and it was enough to keep them pensive for a while.

One of the townsfolk, a woman in a business suit, stumbled up to the officer, blonde hair matted and lank.

'Thank God you're here,' she whispered.

'I'd rather not be here, Miss,' the police officer said without taking his eyes away from the wall of beasts in front of them.

'What the hell happened?' Dean asked.

'These things came from nowhere,' the officer said, jaw squared and mouth clenched. 'A few at first, then the street was full of 'em. It's as if—'

'What?' Dean pressed.

The officer didn't get chance to elaborate. The woman in the business suit began to groan, her hands going to her stomach. Within moments her moan became a scream and across the street the creatures barked an excited answer.

Dean looked down at the woman as she fell to her knees. As she raised her head to the heavens, the long blonde hair slid from her scalp with a hideous sucking sound; the mane slapped wetly onto the cobblestones and lay there like roadkill in a ditch.

The eyes were no longer blue gems; they were pus yellow and weeping violet tears.

'Help her,' another man said. He was short and bald and his eyes were wild with fear. 'She's dying.'

Realisation fell upon Dean like an anvil.

'She's not dying,' he said, stepping away from her. 'She's changing!'

'Into what?' the bald man asked.

'Into one of those things,' the police officer said.

'How is that possible?' Dean hissed.

'That's for another time,' the police officer said.

The woman's mouth was now a snarling maw, her chin on her chest, the jawbone popping with the strain of it. The bones underneath her face seemed to be shifting and made her pale skin ripple like concrete in a quake.

The officer stepped up and placed the pistol on an undulating brow and pulled the trigger. The misshapen skull came apart and cerebral matter fell like heavy rain.

This final shot appeared to be a catalyst for the other creatures, the way a starting pistol signals the start of a race. Fear ate their fury and they came en masse, and not even the pistol could halt the advance. Any hope, any faith, he'd had in man's ability to make a stand was woefully misguided. The police officer—the last sentinel—was bowled over and set upon by several creatures, his uniform clawed away, his skin with it, his abdomen opened and emptied out into the gutter as his screams cleaved the air. The crowd, who stood briefly behind him, turned and ran, Dean mixed in with them, jostled and poked with elbows, shins scraped by flying feet. His hip protested as he limped along, but adrenaline kept it quiet for a while.

Fear herded them, like cattle fleeing from a barn fire, and Dean had the good sense to peel away from them. Not at first. No, he needed to have a few people behind him, slower people. Those people who could be taken in preference to him. It was a shameful act but he could not consider anything other than staying alive.

He passed a middle-aged man who reached out for him, and tried to grasp his shirt.

'Help me,' the man gasped. 'I can't go on!'

Dean slapped at the man's hands as they tried to grab his clothing.

'I'm sorry,' he yelled. 'There's nothing I can do!'

The man went down. And as he heard the cry of pain, Dean wept for what he had lost that day. Humanity was now polarised in the name of survival. He was no less a mindless animal than the things chasing him down.

Then he saw an opportunity. A small alleyway appeared to his left, an access point to the two shops either side of it. He ran as if he intended to pass it, and part of him—the part that didn't want to find itself trapped in a dead end—almost took him past the opening. He veered and ran into the alley, the gloom welcoming after the vivid colours of offal and gore.

His footfalls were big as they reverberated around the high, dank walls. The bricks were a murky brown which added to the gloom. Sheets of discarded newspaper wafted in his wake.

Dean's search for an exit took him deeper into the alley. His heart pummelled his ribs and his throat tasted like metal.

Something entered the alleyway with a deep growl.

He turned to see yellow eyes coming toward him like the headlamps of a car about to strike a paralysed rabbit. The thing had human form and moved slowly, stalking him. Or was it apprehension, uncertainty, after the defiant actions of the police officer?

Despite his fear, Dean processed the sight and tried to rationalise the process. Was this newcomer a human being who had recently gone all the way and transformed like the woman with the blonde hair had tried before she got a bullet in the brainpan?

Dean decided he didn't really care. He just wanted out! Several crates and bin bags lay about him. The air had a faint putrid edge to it and he couldn't be sure if it was the perfume of decay or the creature coming his way.

When Dean saw the fire escape leading to the roof he almost yelled out with joy. He forced himself to remain quiet and edged in the direction of the set of ladders bolted to the far wall. He needed to move fast, to get up the ladders, and gain some advantage. Any sudden movement would have the beast charging at him, and he only had one shot at mounting the rungs fast enough to evade those awful claws.

The fire escape inched painfully closer, and the creature's advance was equally measured. Dean was within three feet of his bid for freedom when three other creatures entered the alleyway and all hell broke loose.

At their approach, the beast that had been stalking him moved fast. It came at him, closing the space between them with frightening efficiency. With a yelp, Dean ran for the ladders, leaping after several steps, arms outstretched and the hatchet still in his right hand. This saved him. The hatchet's head found the third rung and Dean allowed it to take his weight for a few seconds. And, in those few seconds, he was off of the ground, hauling himself up the stave, the hatchet swinging wildly as he sought purchase.

But far from stabilising his actions, the hatchet shifted. Then it wasn't attached to the rung any more. He fell, still tuned in to the sounds about him. A snarl and a cracking sound culminated in a heavy thump. Then something tumbled past him.

He fell six feet and landed on his back amid the pile of black bin bags, their misshapen carcasses disgorging contents under the pressure. Cardboard boxes and soggy papers spilled out, as well as a small stockpile of spent tin cans that clattered away into the alleyway's dark recesses. He was disorientated and winded for a few seconds, but otherwise unharmed.

For now at least.

The creature that had made a lunge for him lay on its side only a few feet away. It showed no sign of life. Then he understood.

During his unceremonious tumble from the ladders his pursuer had made a leap for him just before the hatchet had lost its hold on the rung and he'd collapsed. He quickly looked up and saw there was a smear of blood where the creature, unable to stop once committing to the leap, had cracked its head open on the wall. A few bricks were also caved inwards.

He gingerly climbed to his feet, all too aware that more creatures were en route and eager to make their acquaintance with his flesh. He searched for the hatchet but it was nowhere to be seen and he had no time to look with conviction.

He reached for the fire escape and began to climb, his actions frantic as the noise of the beasts nearby filled the alleyway. His leg throbbed, his shoulder came out in sympathy, but he scaled the steel stairway as fast as he could.

The guttering above served as a proximity marker. He used it to spur himself on. Within moments he was reaching up for the roof.

Then, without warning, something wrenched the ladder away from the wall.

* * *

The ladder was pulled from its base at a forty degree angle, the brackets securing it to the wall squealing loudly before shearing away. Dean didn't waste time. He used the new incline to steady himself and jumped onto the roof, rolling several times before hitting a skylight. The terrible sound of buckling metal came from behind as the ladder was wrenched free of its moorings and smashed into the alleyway below.

He lay on his back briefly, taking stock and getting back his breath. In those moments, he closed off the shocking images he'd seen and considered instead the options that remained open.

The flat roof contained little more than a few TV satellite dishes and seagull shit. The skylight was a possibility, but Dean had no intention of hitting the streets in daylight. He'd barely come away in one piece as it was; handing himself to those things on a plate was not on the menu. Not EVER.

Dean fished around for his cell phone but none of his pockets were forthcoming. He cursed and told himself not to expect anything less; gaolers like Green and his cronies were not likely to allow him access to a cell in his *cell*.

He climbed to his feet and looked at the view, turning a full three-sixty to establish perspective. The sea was smooth, a contrast to the storm taking place upon the shore. As Dean rotated to face inland, the catastrophic truth became apparent.

Smoke smudged the sky and the small streets were littered with bodies that were being defiled by creatures. People were running; their exodus hopeless as the speed and determination of their assailants cut any hope of escape short with clinical efficiency.

As Dean watched it all, he realised only one thing. He'd been lucky to escape at all.

Very lucky.

* * *

Dean was caught in a process. This process was called associated thinking. And in the relative, albeit temporary, safety of the rooftop, the events of that day found time to pierce the flimsy wall he'd built to suppress them, and spilled into his consciousness.

Tears came first. He wept for the people he'd seen butchered: men, women and children; their lives meaningless to the things from Green's lab. When he thought of the errant doctor, the tears became the placards of anger, hot and furious, his face twisted with rage.

The process swept him along as the thoughts of the association between doctor and monster stirred the waters. What the hell had Green created? How the hell were they able to become people? Were they infected with some kind of virus; was this a disease that had eluded a petri dish and sought to reap vengeance on the world? Was all of this too far-fetched and sooner or later a director on some big-budget Hollywood movie would shout 'cut!' and the world would become normal again?

Questions, so many of the fucking things they filled his head until the weight of them brought him to his knees. There were no answers, no way to dig a channel and give release to their insistence.

He continued to sob, trying to find some kind of hope, a way out of the vile mess through which he had to wade. And there had been a flicker of hope, right? The police officer and the handgun, prove positive that the things wreaking havoc on humanity were vulnerable. They could be defeated. The weapons of man would, could be his saviour. The will to survive would be the testament to the tools of destruction. Guns would become God for a short time as man purged the earth of the hellish creatures bent on his destruction.

Weapons.

Association again. His hatchet was lost back in the alleyway, but the police officer had shown how to easily dispatch their foe. His only chance to get out of Gullcrest alive was to find something that spat bullets. With caution and the darkness as his ally he'd get to his car and wheelspin his way to freedom.

He stood, using his bearings, hoping beyond hope that he could get to the police station without having to alight from the roof. He saw chimneys and TV dishes and weather vanes shaped as gulls. Then he saw the mast. It rose from the rooftop landscape like a netted finger pointing to the heavens; three hundred yards away and on his side of the street.

A thump sucked all thoughts from his mind and pumped in fear. He turned to the sound. The skylight, a square of Perspex with meshed glass, jolted upwards as something struck it.

He stepped away as the skylight lifted again, only its security retainer preventing it from flying open. But the glass became a spider-web of cracks.

He skulked away, knowing what was coming for him and certain that the barrier would buy him only meagre portions of time to put in some distance. As he ran, he realised a few home truths, a few realities, of his method of escape.

You're going to run out of roof, Deano. Maybe not soon, but at some point there will be an alleyway and you'll have to jump ten fucking feet to get to the other side. And you ain't no Greg Rutherford, you gettin' me?

Anger held the errant thoughts below the surface, until they became weak, and despite bubbles of reticence breaking to the surface, he was able to concentrate on evading his pursuers.

As his feet hit the bitumen, Dean heard the crashing of the skylight giving in under the barrage of blows from below. Then the air was corrupted with hideous barks and snarls and the din of lumbering feet.

He continued his haphazard, lolloping escape but, as he saw the looming gap of an alleyway separating one building from the next, he had the nagging sensation that he wasn't just running out of roof.

Time was running on empty, too.

* * *

The fact Dean had calculated the probability that he'd have to navigate the space between buildings did take some of the indecision out of the event. Any residual uncertainty was sent scurrying away into dark corners by the clamour of feral barks coming from nearby. So, rather than slow down, Dean accelerated as best he could, keeping his eyes ahead, and using a TV satellite dish on the building opposite as a focal point.

He ran, took a thin breath into lungs that were already aching in protest, and launched himself into free space, arms outstretched and fingers wriggling like an excited child reaching out for a toy.

He wanted to close his eyes, to shut out the fact he was now forty feet up from an unyielding cobblestone alleyway, in the dead air between buildings, and gravity was doing its thing and bringing him down to Earth in more ways than one.

He'd propelled himself forwards enough, and the building he'd just left behind was higher than the one he so desperately needed to receive him. Yet the air gave way to his mass and the brick-lined horizon began to rise as he descended. His arms managed to snake out as his chest hit the side of the building, fingers scrabbling for anything to halt his slide into the alleyway below. His fingertips were skinned by the gritty bitumen sheets but the pain from this was secondary to the need to survive. He locked both elbows into an untidy V and used his armpits to take the strain of his weight. He used his feet to find any anomalies that could be used to push him upwards and relieve some of the strain on his fragile shoulder.

His right loafer found the crumbling mortar between weathered bricks and he pushed down hard in combination with his forearms. He hauled himself upwards until the edge of the roof folded him in the middle, and his bruised chest was pressed into the gnarled surface with his legs still hanging in free space.

Dean lay there panting, not quite believing what he'd achieved. He was shuffling forwards and bringing his legs back onto terra firma when something slapped against the side of the building. Instinctively he snapped his head left.

And found only the black, black eyes of his hunter.

* * *

At the back of his mind, Dean felt a degree of pride in the fact that, despite its formidable physical capabilities, the creature still had not been able to clear the roof. There may have been a variety of reasons for this, but none of them took precedence over his scream as the thing reached out for him.

Dean rolled away, his legs still jutting out over the roof at the knee. He addressed this by scrabbling up to his feet. He was about to start running as best he could when the realisation that he wasn't capable of putting the kind of distance needed to still maintain an advantage settled in. He'd be caught within seconds and torn to pieces in possibly even less time.

Instead, he turned to face his assailant as the creature flailed its legs to help it scuttle onto the roof. No, his advantage was in the here and now, while the beast concentrated on climbing.

Dean ran up to it. The creature lifted its head to snarl at his approach, making it easier for Dean to kick it squarely in the face. Bone splintered and his toe sank into an eye socket, popping the orb. Black goo gushed over his loafer as he pulled back his foot.

The creature screamed and the sound was a blend of pain and fury. It still held its position on the roof and, to Dean's horror, its clawed fingers were gouging into the bitumen sheeting. He stepped back and delivered another kick to the creature's face. This time the blow caught the thing in the jaw, cleaving it in half, and the left mandible punctured the skin of the cheek like some twisted root escaping from cold earth.

Still the creature clung on, and soon there was no stopping Dean's anger. He aimed repeated kicks at the exposed head, mashing cheeks, shattering eye sockets, severing the lolling tongue which slapped onto the roof with a soggy sound. And, as he vented his rage on the beast, he wept and spat and snarled; the caged fear and revulsion now fuel for a terrible act of catharsis.

By the time the beast was dead, its skull was shaped as a bloodied half-moon. But despite all of the blows it had received, the creature did not once let go of the roof. Even now, in death, its hands remained gripping the rents it had gouged for itself; as though the desire to kill would have always have taken precedence over its own demise.

* * *

Aching and nauseated, Dean made his way across the roof. He stayed clear of any skylights, wary of what may be lurking beneath them. He wasn't in any shape to outrun another of those things so soon. What he needed was to get to the police station, find a way to communicate to the outside world.

But then what, Deano?

This made him pause. Indeed, 'then what'. Was he to stay put and wait for rescue? Or continue with the idea of waiting until dark and getting back to his car?

The mast indicating the police station was only one hundred yards away, but Dean didn't know what to expect when he got inside the building. It may have been overrun by the beasts. It was too early to make clear decisions of 'then what'.

Far too early.

He moved again, trying to ignore his discomfort. His hip throbbed and his shoulder ached like fuck. The natural pain relief provided by adrenalin was wearing off. He grimaced with each step and his chest hurt like a son of a bitch.

It was slow going but he soon found himself in the shadow of the police mast, the sun casting crazy zigzags across his face. The mast rose from an upended, rectangular structure that was painted dark grey, save for a white door that lay ominously open. Beyond the door was a slab of darkness. It made Dean slow up and he finally stopped a few feet away. He listened out for any kind of movement.

Nothing.

Dean proceeded warily and slowed down on the threshold. He peered into the building. In the gloom was a small landing leading to a set of stairs. The concrete floor was stained with old blood that creaked and slurped as he stepped through it with his loafers.

A few days ago he would have found such an undertaking revolting. But too much bloody water had passed under the bridge and this became what it was, a means to an end. And that end would be freedom.

He began to walk down the steps, his face screwing up each time his footfalls created a shuffling echo that seemed intent on giving him away. Every so often he would stop and cock his head to one side, straining to hear anything that would indicate he was in danger. After two flights of stairs he came to a door. It was solid with a small glass panel at head height. The door was propped open and Dean's heart began piston-pumping; the object preventing the door from closing was a human head.

It belonged to a man. The eyes were wide and sightless; one was staring at him, the other rolled back so that only the white was visible. The mouth was wide, as though frozen in an eternal scream, and three of the upper teeth, one fang and two incisors, were missing, possibly lost as the heavy door tried to close.

When he got closer, he saw that the head was still attached to the remnants of a body. He peeked through the gap in the door. The torso was naked and ruined, making it difficult to determine if this was the body of a police officer or a visitor.

Deftly, Dean pulled open the door and stepped through, this time making sure to avoid the entrails in his path. He wrinkled his nose at the stink of old meat and circumvented the body to enter a small corridor with bland walls and several doors ahead.

Unless circumstances had improved his chances, he wouldn't find guns in the building. Home office protocols stipulated that firearms were to be stored in a specialist safe secured inside an armed response vehicle. He'd have to find the parking compound and keys to such a vehicle. The task wasn't going to be easy but that was only going to be in keeping with the rest of his day so far.

Dean crept down the corridor. The doors were solid and painted deep cream. Each had a pane of mesh glass that allowed him to peer into the offices beyond and check if they were clear. The rooms were uniform: grey filing cabinets stood alongside a few beech wood desks with computers sitting on them; the walls were covered in a mixture of crime prevention literature and leaflets.

Dean searched a few desk drawers but his efforts became half-hearted after three offices yielded nothing. As he entered the last office, his investigation adopted a different focus. The room had more space, and only a single, weighty desk at one end of the room. There were chairs, one behind the desk, two in front of it. The door held a plaque which told him the office belonged to the chief constable.

This was to become immaterial to proceedings when Dean saw the building schematic on the wall. It was laminated and its flat surface glistened like wet skin. He went to it. A small red dot stuck onto the drawing revealed his current location. Dean placed a finger on the map, and traced it along linear corridors and stairways, reading the numbers and corresponding descriptors listed underneath the drawing.

His gaze alighted on one particular room.

Duty room.

After a quick period of orientation Dean continued to scrutinise the schematic and found the access route to the car park, in essence a secure compound at the centre of the building.

Satisfied, he left the office and began his journey, his mind keen, the schematic a beacon in his head. He navigated another set of stairs, the walls magnolia and blank, his need to find a means of defending himself driving him, giving him confidence. As he arrived on the ground floor landing, the bloody smears on the wall gave him some perspective, a reminder that the world was no longer as it should be.

Dean carefully opened the door that gave way to the ground floor. He revisited the mental schematic in his head. If he went left it would take him to the cells—right, to the duty room where keys to the compound and the ARVs most likely waited for him.

As he turned right, his foot caught something, sending it skittering across the corridor before clattering loudly against the wall.

'Shit!' he said in surprise and winced as the waste paper bin rolled to a stop several feet away.

He looked both ways, bracing himself for the potential consequences his carelessness may have caused. But rather than the crashing, snarling racket of Green's offspring, another sound came to him.

'Hello? Hello? Can you help me? Please! Get me out of here!'

The small and insistent pleas were coming from his left.

From the direction of the cells.

* * *

The voice left Dean off-kilter. His immediate thought was to ignore it. This was instantaneously snuffed out as morality kicked its way into the room. A journalist with a conscience; who would've thought it, let alone believe it?

'You there? Anyone?' The voice again, hesitant this time. Uncertain.

Dean looked at the access door. It was a great grey slab of bland steel, but it was thrown wide open. As he walked through it he saw four similar doors. They had drop-down hatches that served as observation panels and, if the occupant was unpredictable, space through which a tray of food could be served.

Dean knew all of this before he'd even seen the cells. One didn't play hard and fast with Ol' Jim without making the acquaintance of a cell or two. And, in Dean's case, there were times when, if he'd spent any more time sleeping off a bender at Her Majesty's pleasure, he'd have earned a loyalty card.

'Where are you?' he said, his voice hushed.

'Here!' The voice was back with renewed vigour.

A small, pale arm snaked out through the hatch of the second cell door and waved; the hand tiny and fervent.

'Hang on, I'm coming,' he said. Dean moved quickly, reaching the door in a few seconds. He peered into the hatch and found himself looking at a girl and the sight of her made him freeze like a rabbit in danger. She was around nine years of age, her black shoulder-length hair was an unkempt thatch, and she wore a faded "Take That" T-shirt and combat pants.

Her thin face was pale and blotched from crying. Even as he watched, tears still ran down her cheeks. But neither her despair nor her predicament had him nailed to the floor, unable to move forwards or retreat.

It was her eyes. Because the corneas of the youth staring at him through the observation hatch were as yellow as the midday sun.

* * *

'Won't you help me?' the girl pleaded. Her eyes seemed to pierce him with their insistence, their desire to savour liberty once more.

A wave of dizziness passed through Dean. He used the door frame to steady himself until the sensation left him.

The day is mauling you badly, Deano. It doesn't look like it's quite finished with you yet.

'Who are you?' he asked as the dizziness retreated. He shook his head to help it on its way. 'What the hell happened to you?'

The girl's lip trembled before her face screwed up and a fresh tide of tears spilled from her jaundiced eyes. She tried to stem the flow; the heel of each hand wedged into her sockets, her fingers crisscrossing her brow like a lattice of pink flesh.

Dean took a breath and tried to find some stronghold in a tenuous reality. He found it in a loose form of social conscience. He was an adult and she was a distraught child. It was not his place to add to her woes but to placate them, soothe them, and keep her safe until he could find her parents. Wasn't that what he'd craved for all those years ago, when his bitch of a sister and his spineless father had conspired to turn the world to shit? Hadn't he always wished for someone— anyone—to come to his fucking rescue? No one had come for him. It was his duty to learn from such things. To be better than those who chose to ignore his pleas.

Yeah, but this girl could be one of them, his fear said to him. *She could be—*

'What?' he contested. Damaged? Any more or less damaged than he was as a child—even now? Would he really let history repeat itself and walk away without finding some way to learn from his own hell? Wasn't it laudable to just fucking try to help?

He looked up at her, past her, and into the cell she had made her own in the absence of choice. Drawings were tacked to the walls, images of a small girl holding hands with a tall man in a white coat. Surprised, he also noted other pictures that had more people dressed in decontamination suits and gas masks, and the same small image looking up at them with a half-moon smile. A small bunk served as a bed and art studio, a pencil case and paper lay on a flimsy cotton sheet. Wrappers were piled neatly in another corner, crisps and snack bars, the staple diet of the exiled.

The contained.

'Look,' he said as softly as he could. 'Please don't cry. I will help you. Do you hear me? I will help you.'

The girl took in a shuddering sniff as she peeled her hands away from her eyes.

'Do you mean that?' The air of mistrust was blatant.

'Yes,' he emphasised. 'I promise. I just need to know that you're okay.'

'I'm not okay,' she said sharply. 'I've been locked in here for hours.'

'Okay, okay,' he said in an attempt to calm her. 'I can understand you're pissed off—I mean, upset, but I have to go and find the keys to this cell so I can let you out.'

'No!' she cried, stepping up to the hatch. 'You won't come back! You'll leave me in here because I'm weird! Just like the rest of them! Just like Daddy!'

'No, I won't,' he assured her. 'Listen, what's your name?'

'Susan,' she said.

Dean's heart did a leap and attempted to crawl up his gullet. 'Susan?'

'Yes.'   Her golden stare was a stark contrast to her sullen expression. 'Susan Hadley.'

* * *

It was turning into a day of wonders. Some repugnant, some remarkable, but all were challenging a journalist's views on what constituted normality. The true focus of his search was here, standing in a cell, peering at him with golden eyes through a slot framed in grey steel.

'But how?' he whispered. 'How can you be here?'

Susan shrugged and the movement accentuated her youth. Dean instantly felt foolish and changed his approach by softening his demeanour.

'Listen, Susan,' he said. 'You've been missing for over two years, right? People have been looking for you. The police. Everyone. People thought you'd drowned.'

'I haven't been anywhere,' she said as her face morphed in confusion. 'I've been here.'

'Here? In this cell?' Dean asked.

'No, silly!' Susan said with an unexpected giggle. It was a sound that said adults can be so stupid. 'In Gullcrest.'

'Susan,' Dean said slowly, as if trying to talk to someone who perhaps did not have the capacity to understand his words. 'Your parents have probably been worried sick. They probably thought you were—'

He stopped. But this wasn't because his intended words had the potential to upset or inflame an already difficult situation. A thought glided through his head. A thought that had him changing direction and moving away from questions about parents hiding behind the tune of "Ten Green Bottles" whenever people were asked. Susan interrupted his deliberations.

'Parents? My mother died some years ago,' she said. It was the tone of a child who didn't have a reference point; she used the term 'mother' as a word with no emotional context. She spoke as someone who didn't know what it really meant.

'So who were you with, Susan?'

'Daddy,' she said simply. 'In his lab.'

Dean's world wavered for a few seconds as he deciphered and digested her explanation.

'Professor Green is your father?'

'Yes.'

'But the surname?' His mind craved understanding. 'It's different.'

'Yes.' She sighed as though bored. 'Hadley was my mother's maiden name. Daddy gave it to me to honour her. That's what he told me anyway. I don't remember her at all.'

'But what were you doing at the lab?' he asked. 'For these past few years?'

'I have a disease,' she said as she cast her gaze downwards for a few seconds. Dean said nothing. He knew embarrassment when he saw it. He owned a mirror after all. 'It's an illness that makes me grow old too fast.'

She sounded like a bad actress reading from a poor script, voice monotone, the sentences flowing as those recited a thousand times and still not making any emotional connection with them.

'Progeria?'

'Yes,' she said. 'I think that's what Daddy calls it.'

As she spoke, Dean was taken back to the journal in Green's lab and things, that for so long had become disjointed, began to morph back into shape. Sure, it was still unfamiliar and had limited cogency but it painted a clearer picture than it had only moments before.

It referred to the section of red script where the professor claimed he'd found a cure.

'The regenerative enzyme P138 is a success! The results from Subject 37 conclude substantive moderation of the Lamin A protein. Progeria, this accused disease, is in its final moments. Soon I must turn my intentions to the scientific casualties about me. It is a necessary evil in order to expound the boundaries of knowledge. People may not understand my methods but perhaps, in time, they may understand my motives. What father would not?'

What father would not? Indeed, Professor. Indeed.

'So your father tried to make you better, right?'

'He said he'd found a way to make me better,' she said. 'He injected me with something. A green liquid.'

'In the lab?'

'Not the first time,' she replied. 'At our home. But he had to go back to his lab and said I had to go with him so I could be monitored. I didn't understand at first. Then the men in white explained it all. Daddy needed to keep an eye on me because there were lots of injections and he needed me to be safe.'

The girl being abducted in the rain, Deano, Jenna said. *The one who gave you the code to the fucking lab. She's standing here in front of you but that's not the jaw dropper, is it? What's yanking your chain is how the fuck did you dream about it? How did you know?*

He shut Jenna out. Now wasn't the time for such things. The town was overrun and he had a potentially infected child in a cell. Decisions had to be made; let her out and wait for her to turn batshit or leave her in the cell to take her chances?

'So how did you end up in here?' he asked. 'Where is your father now?'

'I was feeling better after lots of injections,' she recalled. 'The wrinkles on my face disappeared. I didn't ache anymore; I could move my arms and legs. All my hair grew back.'

He sensed pride as she recounted her recovery. He recalled the sketches of sufferers in Green's journal.

'Then what?' he pushed her.

'Then my eyes turned to this horrid colour,' she whispered. 'And Daddy got angry. He left me in my room to go back to his lab. He didn't come back for several hours and then when he did it was to tell me we had to leave. He said that things had gotten out of hand.'

Dean smiled grimly. Not only was the professor a maverick genius but he had also coined the greatest understatement of the twenty-first century. His mutants were running amok in the streets of his home town and his daughter was locked in a police cell.

'How long have you been like this, Susan?' he asked carefully.

'A few days,' she said, sniffing back tears.

'You mean that you've been here at the station for two days? Locked in here?'

'Yes,' she conceded. 'Daddy and his men brought me here for my own protection. He knows the chief constable. They're old friends.'

A good enough friend to cover up a missing child, perhaps? And in a position to feed the press bullshit about a drowned girl? Maybe, but that was one for another lifetime.

'Look,' he said. 'I'm going to try and find some keys, okay? I'll be a few minutes and I'll come back for you.'

'That's what they said after they locked me in here!' she protested.

'Look,' he said firmly. His sharp tone stopped her. 'There are worse things out here.' His voice eased a little. 'At the moment you're safe, protected. You need to trust me, okay? I'll come back, I promise.'

He meant it. But he'd made a point not to promise that he'd let her out. The hunt for keys would buy him time to see if she would change into one of those things slaughtering innocents in the streets outside. Chances were she'd be okay. There was no sign of violent tendencies or a desire to chew his face off, all a good sign.

'Ten minutes, okay?' he said to her.

Her face told him she wasn't happy about it but she nodded once. She even managed a smile but the golden eyes detracted from it and added to the surreal quality of events.

'Back soon,' he said and left before either had a chance to change their minds over what would happen next.

* * *

He found the key rack in a large room several doors from the cell bay. The keys were hanging on their exposed hooks as soon as he entered. His moment of triumph was diluted as the smell of rotting offal hit him and he took in the human remains sprawled across one of the desks. The body was face down and innards had been ripped out through its back, the spinal column wrenched upwards where it stood erect like some macabre dodgem car conduit.

Another mauled figure lay on the floor a few feet away from him. The arms had been ripped away from their sockets and discarded, lost to view. The face was nothing but a ragged hole where churned meat and splintered bone glistened like jewels at the touch of the sunlight through the window.

Dean navigated the desks and bodies in order to get to the key rack. The carpets were sticky with blood. These kills weren't exactly fresh but close enough to remain a stark warning that the creatures could vent their rage at any time, in any place.

Each key was numbered and Dean deciphered the code list pinned next to the rack. He grabbed the keys to the cell, then those for an ARV. As he turned to exit the office, the green first aid box planted on a small table behind the office door caught his eye.

He went to it and carefully pried the lid apart, grabbing a pack of paracetamol which he cracked open. He dry-swallowed four pills, not bothering to check the dosage, and hoped the pain-killing relief it brought to his shoulder and hip would be worth the vile, bitter taste they left in his throat. He pocketed the packet and left the office for the cells.

Dean wasn't sure exactly when he'd decided that he was going to set Susan free. His instincts took him back to her cell and he courted no further thought as to how good or bad an idea it might prove. He entered the cell bay, and began prepping to use the keys to release the girl. What he found there showed him the day wasn't done with throwing curve balls.

The door to Susan's cell was wide open.

* * *

'Shit!'

Anxiety was sending his muscles into spasm, his belly to ice water. He was torn between slinking off, unseen and relatively safe, or keeping a promise to a frightened child that he would come back and protect her.

Get the fuck out of here, Deano! Jenna again. *You owe her nothing! Fuck, she could even be one of those things!*

Humanity is turning sour. Do I really want to help drag it into the sunlight where it can turn to cheese that much faster? Do I want to leave a child, frightened and alone, without even checking she's okay?

Want her to rip out your throat and play skip-rope with your guts, Deano?

Fuck you, sis! Just fuck right off!

'Susan?' His voice was water thin. 'Are you okay?'

He dragged his feet forward, the smooth floor tiles making the transition easier than his legs would have hoped. For some reason his arm was bent at a right angle, the key ready yet redundant. There was no sound other than that of his loafers squeaking on the linoleum. No indication that Susan was now a savage creature bent on ripping open his belly.

But he wasn't going to take any more chances than needed.

Dean put his back against the wall, the doorjamb inching ever closer. He hauled in a breath and slowly peered into the cell.

It was empty.

* * *

Dean raced through the corridors. Part of him was intrigued as to how Susan had escaped the cell, but another part saw this as another mystery that increased the chances of him ending up dead. There were no signs that the door had been forced. That meant two things: someone had opened it or it had never been locked in the first place. At that moment, Dean couldn't see anything good in either scenario.

Perhaps I'll feel differently when I've a Glock 17 in my hand.

Dean found the entrance to the parking compound pretty quickly. Several police vehicles were in a large, open space. The perimeter was walled and, in the far corner, was a security exit; his way out of this mess.

The key to the ARV made things simple. The chunky black fob had the car registration etched into its plastic surface; Dean already knew that ARVs were easily distinguishable from standard police patrol cars by their solid silver and orange markings. There were two such vehicles parked up next to each other. One of them already had its boot thrown open, an event that had Dean recalling the image of the police officer pumping bullets into the creatures as they charged the crowded streets.

Dean pressed the fob and the other ARV bleeped at him, its lights blinking twice. He opened the boot and look in, spotting the safe immediately and his heart sank as he saw the combination key pad lying dormant, yet expectant, in the centre of the ebony steel surface.

'Shit,' he mouthed. 'You gonna give me a break sometime soon?' He said it to no one in particular and wasn't expecting any kind of response. Yet an idea did drop into his head. It wasn't so much divine intervention as desperation.

Moving to the next ARV he looked at the gun locker and found it open. Daring not to hope for too much he reached in and his hand found two hand guns, which he carefully withdrew. There were also magazines, six in total. He laid these out in the boot.

Glock 17s were standard issue. Each clip contained nine nineteen-millimetre bullets and Dean figured he'd need them all to get clear of the town. Not that he expected too much in way of opposition, it was just a conservative view on his skills of using a hand gun.

Many years ago he'd written a piece for the paper on gun violence. As part of this he'd spent three days with the local constabulary. There he'd learnt how to shoot, just to give him insight into the power of wielding a firearm and how this might inform the mindset of those who were both disaffected and socially impotent. It was a good lesson, but the upshot meant he was a shit shot. Even after the three days of extensive training.

Hell, the reality was he would fare better running Green's bastard offspring down with the ARV. Having the guns was still a comfort, and he clumsily slammed in the clip and chambered a round into each weapon, his memory creaking through the process.

The splintering of wood and bright tinkle of glass hitting asphalt helped him focus. He twirled to face the direction from which the destructive sounds came and was in time to see three creatures powering through a door across the yard. One of them cleaved the barrier in two as it broke into the compound. Such was its momentum, the beast ploughed into a parked sedan and rolled over it, leaving behind an imprint of its hideous form in the car's bodywork.

The creature barked as it climbed to all fours, its misshapen head turned towards Dean, who stood there, a Glock held out in each trembling hand.

The creature stood erect, flanked by its two companions, both smaller but no less hostile. A trio of salivating mouths waited to ruin his flesh, longing to savour it between their powerful jaws.

As he watched the creatures advance, Dean found himself searching for the exact point where it had all gone so wrong.

Nothing, other than the three growling creatures, came to him.

* * *

Dean aimed both guns at the larger creature. There was method to this as a concept. If he took out the biggest, the strongest, the others would flee. He'd seen how wary the beasts were of the police officer.

You gotta hit the fucking thing first, Deano, Jenna sneered. *In the head. And what are fucking odds of you doing that before these things decide to turn you inside out?*

He squinted down the barrel of the Glock in his right hand. It jittered in his grasp, his palm slick with sweat and gun grease. Anxiety sent a moist curtain of rivulets down his brow.

Concentrate, Dean. Just concentrate.

He had to squeeze the trigger; he remembered that part from his training. The gunshot was loud and, even though he'd prepped for it, he flinched at the recoil.

The bullet ripped through the air and the creatures were startled by the enormous sound. The big beast took the bullet in its shoulder where a hole appeared and dumped green blood down its chest.

'Fuck me,' Dean breathed. 'I hit it.'

But not in the head, shit shot, Jenna said. *Now they're gonna use your guts for spaghetti. Yes, they're gonna slurp them down real good.*

The gunshot was replaced with a roar of pain and rage. The three creatures bore down on him, the biggest in the lead, now only twenty feet away. In panic, Dean opened up with the Glock, but this time the shots did not hit home. He put holes through four office windows and took out a car headlight. The creatures were so close he could smell their rank, butcher-shop reek which came to him like a rancid perfume, making his eyes water. The Glock clicked empty and Dean discarded it as he swapped hands. He squeezed the trigger again.

Nothing happened.

The beast was ten feet away, companions hard on its malformed heels. Dean's belly was a sudden ball of ice and he wanted to piss badly. He tried again and still the Glock remained impotent.

Check your trigger guard, moron, Jenna said.

He risked looking down at the gun. His finger was trying to press the guard not the trigger.

'Shit!'

Dean adjusted his wayward digit just as the large beast launched itself at him. Dean's world was filled with the sight of vicious, misshapen teeth, and a leering skull-mask. He brought up the weapon and opened, six bullets reworking the creature's head into a new shape.

Dean was bowled over as the carcass hit him, gore slopping onto his legs and feet. Dean landed on his back. He fought to keep his grip on the gun as the creature's companions pulled up and eyed him with barely contained fury. As he'd suspected, they wanted to chow down on him but they were afraid; the fear may have been buried deep, yet it was enough for them to halt.

Dean scrambled to his feet, thankful the paracetamol had dulled the pain in his hip and shoulder enough for him to keep moving. He kept the gun trained on his adversaries as he dug deep into his pockets and pulled out the fob for the ARV.

He wasn't delusional, though at that moment in time he really wished all of this was nothing more than a mind-bender, and he was not really in a police compound doing battle with crazed mutants.

Instead, he was rocking backwards and forwards on some mental health unit, waiting for the Olanzapine to kick in. He knew he got lucky taking out their leader, and the odds of successfully testing that luck were poor. He needed to get in the car and make a run for it. Choices were as few as his remaining bullets, after all.

Dean ran for the ARV and the creatures were spurred into action by the realisation that their prey was trying to evade them. He got to the passenger door and yanked it open, diving into the car and slamming it shut just before one of the creatures smashed it inwards, shattering the window and tilting the vehicle on its chassis.

The head that pushed through the jagged pane was so intent on introducing its mouth to Dean's body; it seemed impervious to the glass slicing into its livid flesh. Black, lifeless eyes sought him out, bulbous and cupped by sockets of maroon meat.

Dean lay on his back, sprawled across the two seats, as he tried to put distance in a cramped space. The Glock came up, and Dean put a bullet through the creature's right eye. Black jelly spewed onto the upholstery and the thing fell backwards, tumbling from view.

His ears ringing, Dean manipulated his body into the driving seat, rammed the key into the ignition and was immediately aware that a shadow had fallen across the windscreen. The last monster was making its presence known by clambering onto the bonnet, the weight putting divots into the vehicle's skin.

The Glock in his lap, Dean fired up the engine and slammed the car into first. He might not be the best shot but he wasn't as inept when it came to driving. His confidence returned; the car was now his weapon of choice. The vehicle shot forward, his would-be nemesis sent pin wheeling onto the roof. Overhead something solid hit the bodywork and the alternating flasher unit hit the asphalt to his right where it exploded like a small blue-and-red bomb.

In his rear-view mirror, Dean had the satisfying sight of the beast bouncing across the compound in a tangle of arms and legs, its body brutalised by impact trauma. Once it had stopped rolling it lay still, blood pumping out onto the white lines marking the bays.

Dean powered the big engine and the ARV smashed into the security gate, knocking it aside with remarkable ease. He pulled the wheel left and the car traversed the street with a squeal of tyres and blue-grey smoke. The driver's side front wheel clipped the kerb and sent the trim spinning into a waste bin, felling it like a tree and allowing the contents to be dragged into the air by the breeze.

Dean straightened the ARV and accelerated. He headed west, searching for a way out of town. Signposts told him he needed to take a right at the end of the street. On either side, stores with brightly coloured awnings waited to lure tourists, but now they were nothing more than shattered shells, their contents spilling out onto the pavement.

Dean navigated the car through debris born from disorder. Other vehicles were either abandoned, doors left wide, or lying on their sides, discarded like toys in the nursery of a disruptive child.

There were bodies, too. Lots of them; too many to count, mauled and mutilated, ruined carcasses left for the gulls. He checked the rear-view mirror in an attempt to shut out the horrors about him. What he saw there held his attention for a little too long.

A helicopter hovered in the air, its rotors churning up the debris in the street. The machine was white, without markings, and represented many things at that moment: proof positive that the world still turned outside this hell hole, and perhaps this was part of a rescue, a respite in the perpetual assault on mankind.

Then he saw Susan. The girl was running, through the chaos, her black hair whipped by the updraft from the rotors. Behind her, the helicopter was unravelling ropes and figures in biochem suits slid down each umbilical like white beads on a necklace. Once they hit the pavement, they headed after the girl.

In a moment he saw all of this, yet it was still too long. By the time his gaze returned to the road ahead, the post office van was already filling the windscreen. He pulled the wheel hard left and the ABS kicked in, making the chassis shudder beneath his feet. The ARV slewed and struck the post office van on the front quarter and a loud bang filled the air before the car came to a halt.

Dean's head struck the driver's window, the impact putting small galaxies in his head for a few seconds. He let the disorientating effects of the blow pass, his breathing heavy with relief that he'd managed to stay alive. Dean lost grip on the gun and it went tumbling into the foot well.

Dean could hear shouts and cries for help and forced his body to move, unclipping his belt in preparation to leave the vehicle. He opened the car door, and made to step out but his hip gave way and he spilled onto the road.

He looked up and saw Susan running towards him, feet pounding the pavement hard and swift. Behind her one of the figures in the biochem suit went down on one knee and lifted a rifle, taking aim at the retreating girl.

'No!' Dean yelled. 'Don't do it! She's just a kid!'

It was enough to get the sniper's attention. Now the rifle was trained on him.

Great.

Dean tried to climb to his feet, Susan now only fifty feet away. There was a distant pop and a sharp stinging pain caught Dean in the neck.

He slapped a hand to the site, his mouth already going numb. Within seconds he was succumbing to a sensation that was all too familiar.

As he slipped into unconsciousness, he took Susan's frantic screams with him.

* * *

Through the tranquil haze, Dean's stomach lurched as he was lifted into the sky. The world was spinning, and straps pinned him to the gurney as the helicopter made its ascent. The wind was a howling beast, tousling his hair and turning the material of his shirt into fierce ripples. He managed to turn his head and saw Gullcrest in the distance, the buildings small, many of them burning.

Then there was a roar, louder than the wind, impossible to drown out and, as he watched, something streaked beneath them, a silver cylinder trailing grey smoke.

The projectile struck the town and he closed his eyes but still saw the iridescent orb in the darkness. There was a loud crackle and a deep thud. Then, nothing.

When Dean looked back at the shoreline, the town of Gullcrest was now a vast steaming crater in the landscape. He found himself asking what the hell the world was coming to shortly before his doped brain sought respite by shutting down for a while. This time he made no attempt to fight the waves of fatigue. The only thing he did take with him into sweet oblivion was awareness that someone gently stroked his hand.

TWO DAYS AGO

The sun coming in from the window warmed his cool skin. Night sweats were as much a part of his marriage to Ol' Jim as the shakes. All in all, the wet sheets and the trembling fingers were aspects of mourning. Dean kicked the covers onto the floor and fought off a bout of cramp in his right calf by drawing his foot towards his ankle. He got cramps a lot. Someone once told him the build-up of lactic acid in the muscle was exacerbated by alcohol.

That figures.

He pawed at his eyes and coughed hard, dislodging phlegm from his throat before swallowing it. A half-bottle of Ol' Jim stood on the dressing table and he went to make its acquaintance, finishing it with ease. He relished the taste, and his smile gave the emotion form.

'Oh, man,' he said, staring out at the sun-soaked city. 'Some days life is so fucking good, it hurts.'

He showered then made scrambled eggs and toast, coupled with strong coffee. He ate breakfast in silence, save for the noises from the street below. He loved this time of the day, the city alive and bustling, the hopes that a day would yield something different.

Dean grabbed his coat, a beaten-up three-quarter Barbour, its waxed blue weatherproofing smooth to the touch. In one of the pockets was a silver hip flask with a dragon motif, his little shot of comfort while at the office.

He locked the front door and made his way to the elevators. En route, Mrs Marshall came out to check if the postman had left any packages on her welcome mat. He bade her a courteous good morning and she acknowledged him with a brief nod before scuttling back inside, her heavy towelled dressing gown flapping behind her.

The elevator journey was completed in isolation, no stopping on the descent to let anyone in, and Dean filled the silence with a tone deaf rendition of U2's Beautiful Day.

He walked through the foyer and gave Trevor Annison, the concierge, a wave. As usual, Trevor adjusted his bulk and brought two fingers to the tip of his cap in a half-hearted salute.

Unlike breakfast, the journey to work wasn't as usual. People moved with a sense of urgency out of keeping even to that of commuters heading into work. They jostled each other and spat curses as they continued on their way. One middle-aged man in a business suit came close to shoving a young woman in a summer dress and denim jacket into the street after they had a brief altercation over who was and who wasn't looking where they were going.

The queues were within a few hundred metres from his offices, row upon row of fidgeting, impatient people. He paused and followed where the head of each queue ended. Every line seemed to disappear into a shop. Grocers, delicatessens, minimarts, each owned a queue, and those who emerged from such establishments had shoulders sagging under the weight of carrier bags laden with food. The eyes of those still standing in line would follow them as they moved away, and Dean felt uncomfortable with what he saw in those faces.

Envy. Raw and deep.

He shrugged off a hideous sense of foreboding and headed to work. The world was entitled to a crazy day once in a while.

The offices of The Chronicle were on a crossroads. Dean turned left and the familiar sight of the brown brick and steel building as it rose up from the structures around it gave a sense of comfort.

To his left, another crowd queued outside a frozen food store. There were grumbles and short sharp shouts as people accused others of pushing into the line or leaving having taken more than their fair share.

What's going on? Did I miss something? Dean's puzzled thoughts were migrating to the expression on his face.

Another sound was in the air. The rumble of a large truck had Dean turning to see an articulated wagon with RED Co. emblazoned on its tarpaulin. The lorry stopped and the crowds moved urgently towards it.

The back doors opened from the inside and several men in smart red overalls smiled at the pool of people lapping against the truck's rear.

'Rest easy, folks!' one of the men said in a big voice. 'There's plenty for all. I just need you to be patient and orderly.'

Dean watched as each person was given a box, a food parcel of sorts, each marked with a RED Co. label. Bemused, Dean moved away from the scene, leaving the crowds reaching up, a forest of hands yearning for their share.

* * *

Dean's desk was on a mezzanine floor that he accessed via a flight of stairs. The whole floor was open plan with meeting and interview rooms on the periphery. At the centre of the mezzanine was a pod-shaped structure made of glass. Inside, Cound paced like a frustrated pet rodent in its tank.

The editor looked up as Dean started for his desk. Cound came to the door and pulled it open.

'Sharp! Here! Now!' he barked.

'I've got to—'

'Now, dammit!' Cound snapped.

Dean shrugged and went to the pod. After shutting the door, he sat on the visitor's chair parked in front of Cound's big desk.

'What?' His tone was blunt. His day wasn't getting any better, it seemed.

'Where the fuck have you been?' Cound drummed his fingers on his desk and took a gulp of coffee from a huge mug that said 'I'm the Boss, Get over it!'

'You want to run that by me again?' Dean said as confusion danced across his face.

'You've been AWOL for three fucking days.' Cound snorted. 'I'm not here to subsidise another bender, Sharp. You got me?'

'Sounds like I ain't the only one hitting the hard stuff,' Dean said firmly while eyeing the mug. 'You sure that's just coffee?'

'I'm sure,' Cound snapped. 'Though, if anyone is going to have me courting a bottle, it'll be you. You got an explanation? And no bullshit, right?'

Dean stared blankly at his editor, unsure of to how to move forward with this. 'I was here yesterday,' he said weakly.

'You were last here on the seventh,' Cound said. 'It's now the tenth.'

Dean allowed the sickly feeling in his gut a few moments to get comfortable. He checked the date on his watch and it confirmed Cound's perspective.

'I don't know,' Dean said as his body began deflating in the chair. 'I don't know what happened.'

'Another fucking blackout is what's happened, Sharp,' Cound said as he threw his arms up in exasperation. 'If you weren't so fucking good at what you do I'd fire your sorry arse, you know that?'

'Sorry.'

'Yeah, I took that shit ten years ago, don't expect me to do it again,' Cound warned.

'That's low,' Dean replied sullenly. 'That was a bad time for me. You know it.'

'Yes.' Cound sighed. 'I know it. But what do you expect?'

'Some understanding?'

'Like last time?' Cound asked. 'I gave you understanding. I gave you time.'

'Not that it did any good,' Dean said.

'You lost your memory and the south coast lost a town,' Cound recalled. 'And I lost a fuckin' great story. We're all grieving, believe me.'

Cound had never forgiven him for the Gullcrest incident. A town wiped off of the face of the map, an industrial accident by all accounts, and Dean found three miles away, face down on a beach, disorientated and robbed of recall. Ol' Jim, it appeared, had worked his magic in spectacular ways. It had taken all of the editor's resolve not to fire the paper's best reporter on the spot.

'Well, like I said, I'm sorry,' Dean said sourly.

'That still doesn't get me leads, Sharp,' Cound said. 'This thing at the docks is ripping open and spilling out. We've got no angle as of yet. Hell, I thought you'd gone rogue to give us the edge on this bitch.'

The blank expression on his reporter's face caused Cound to stop.

'You've no idea what I'm talking about, right?'

'I'd say that pretty much covers it,' Dean replied.

'You're an embarrassment, you know that?' Cound said. 'We've got a story unfolding here and I got the shareholders crawling up my arse while you go and get shitfaced.'

He pulled a beige Collegiate file from a desk drawer and skimmed it across at Dean.

'Get up to speed and give me an angle within the next hour,' Cound said. 'Or next time you see me I'll be shoving your P45 up your arse, get me?'

Dean told Cound he got him.

Plenty.

* * *

In terms of the story, the contents in the folder filled in the blanks, though Dean suspected the past three days of his life were lost forever. It wasn't the first time such a thing had happened, and it wouldn't be the last, but he was usually aware when a blackout had floored him. He'd wake confused and disorientated, clothes soiled with residual vomit or piss.

Sometimes worse.

Not this time. No, this time he'd woken as if from a deep sleep, with a vague feeling that he'd been dreaming—yet he'd no recollection of what—and as far as he was concerned there had been nothing untoward.

Just like Gullcrest. Shit, why did Cound have to bring that up now? As if things weren't bad enough.

Dean had woken on a beach, sand in his mouth, sea water in his shoes and fuck-all in his head. Well, he remembered driving to the town. He remembered getting out of his MR2 at the Olde Majestic Hotel. After that, not a thing. It had been as though two days had been cut from his brain. When Cound had visited him in hospital hours after Dean had been picked up, the editor had been almost salivating like Pavlov's hounds thinking he had someone on the scene the day a seaside town had been blasted from the face of Earth.

Cound had left disappointed and frustrated, taking away the bag of grapes he'd brought with him. So the public had to make do with the official line: Gullcrest had been destroyed by a build-up of methane gas in one of its sealed-off copper mines. Somehow the gas had ignited and wiped out two miles of landscape and killed a thousand people. Without anyone to contest this position, the story stuck like gum to a sleeve.

Maybe there wasn't anything to tell. Cound wasn't someone who wanted to hear such possibilities. He needed things to sell The Chronicle and bring home the bacon, when he wasn't porking his latest model, of course.

Dean sighed and picked up a piece of paper that had multiple newsfeeds printed across it. The story was intriguing and went some way to explain some of the behaviours he'd witnessed on his way to work that morning.

For some reason, there was a localised food shortage. Bad enough for the home secretary to make an announcement that this was only a short-term issue and advice from the large supermarket outlets was there were plenty of reserves. Such reserves, it seemed, were to be distributed within the week. As such, the public had been advised not to 'panic buy' which had the usual outcome of them doing exactly that the minute the broadcast ended.

The press was speculating, an event that tended to occur when a news blackout was in force; the corridors of power remained closed off to all but those officially paid to walk through them.

One report suggested it wasn't that so much food was not available locally as it wasn't available at all. A year of adverse weather had blighted crops worldwide and resources were generally scarce.

Another suggested that terrorists had somehow found a way to disrupt the distribution chain and speculated that events were akin to Hitler's U-boats cutting off the supply lines during WWII.

Speculation, all of it. Dean could see that from the outset. He trawled through more papers, consisting of news reports and the results of a plethora of internet searches. He couldn't see anything other than a collection of disparate, disjointed items and understood why the bulk of news reports lacked any substance.

He turned to his computer. The screen saver was a rotating image of The Chronicle's letterhead. He hit the mouse and pulled up his desktop, and placed the Alice Cooper cursor on the Internet Explorer icon.

He typed 'UK food distribution centres' into the search box and let the engine do the rest. After scanning the headers, he clicked onto a hyperlink indicating lists of distribution centres through which the UK monitored foodstuff ready to enter the country.

One familiar name kept coming up. Redistribution, Export and Distribution Company or RED Co. for short. He refreshed his search and typed in 'RED Co.' and waited a few seconds.

When the results came up on screen, Dean suspended all thoughts of food shortages and distribution chains. Instead he found himself looking at scandal. Then the journalist within him took over.

* * *

Dean drove his car fast, the low chassis of his Audi hugging the winding road as trees and high hedges zipped by in a blur of green. Ahead the sky was big, the hillside rising to carve a curved horizon into the heavens.

He recalled some of the news articles he'd found online, articles that suggested RED Co. had been very naughty in the past, naughty to the point of having a huge fine imposed upon the company as a whole, and criminal convictions for some of its employees.

RED Co. was more a conglomerate than a company, and had many streams to its business portfolio. It had become too big to watch over all of the small stuff and the crux of the matter seemed its food production arm had gone on a frolic to the detriment of many.

Dean had found that RED Co. was found culpable in the illegal production of genetically modified foods. The site at a small town called Wellington had been closed with immediate effect as the company did its best to evoke damage limitation protocols using corporate lawyers as a buffer. Not only were premises closed but the 'culprits' guilty of 'operating without the knowledge or sanction of RED Co. or any of its subsidiaries or affiliates' were handed over to the police for prosecution.

Now the chief casualty of the whole affair, the closed plant suspected as the origin of the genetically modified produce, lay over the hill on the outskirts of Wellington.

Dean continued on his journey, his mind flitting between the details of the story and the images he'd seen in the streets that morning. The presence of RED Co. trucks distributing free produce to the needy should've been a heart-warming sight—corporate will cast aside for the good of the many. But in truth, having read their spurious history with food handling, Dean was reticent. He didn't discount good intention; a public relations disaster such as the unethical sourcing of illegally manipulated products would take years to undo in the marketplace. Yet, in Dean's experience, people in need were fickle and the appearance of RED Co. trucks dishing out food would find the company executives wading through public Brownie points in no time. He'd seen it first-hand with the truck and the crowds, their faces reverent in the presence of alms. There was no doubt about it, for RED Co., this whole crisis was a PR godsend. Six years out in the wilderness, the corporate pariah was now being welcomed back into the fold. And it wasn't just Ol' Jim that had a habit of dulling the memory. Time was equally as effective at numbing the wily public. RED Co.'s misdemeanours of the past would simply become vague fancies in the minds of the masses.

Just ask any wayward politician.

For Dean it stood up to reason that the fickle, those who needed supplies, would question neither their origins, nor the provider who brought them. But Dean was more curious than most, more paranoid, Jenna would no doubt have said. His sister should know. She was the architect of his neurosis, after all.

* * *

He found the perimeter fence by accident. A few miles out from Wellington, his bladder decided enough was enough and Dean pulled over at a small in-cut that was over grown with tall grass and thistles. A few metres away he found a hedgerow that shielded a row of trees and he intended to use it as cover as he took a piss.

There was a four foot gap between the hedge and the tree line and, as he relieved himself, he spotted a mesh fence, at least ten feet high, lurking beyond the trees. He finished up and went to the fence and, despite only the sounds of birdsong on the air, he still moved with vigilance.

He could see a huge, low structure beyond the fence. It looked like a unit he'd seen many times on industrial estates all over the UK, a dirty brown colour, the elements leaving their mark on its corrugated surface. Here and there, patches of rust and lichen could be seen as swatches of oranges and greens.

Signs tied to the mesh at regular intervals told anyone who cared to read them that the land beyond belongs to RED Co. and trespassers would be prosecuted. Intrigued, Dean decided he would take this under advisement and followed the fence for a few hundred yards before finding a small hole sliced into the mesh. He looked about him, making sure he wasn't being observed, and manoeuvred himself through the gap, cursing as the mesh rattled at his passing.

He got through having snagged the collar of his jacket twice, which resulted in a small scratch on his neck. He rubbed at it but his focus was already turning to the landscape ahead.

Just as with the in-cut, the tarmac standing between the fence and the plant was succumbing to nature. Grass had wormed its way through the asphalt's crumbling skin, and wherever industrial debris had been left, bracken or foliage had laid claim to it. Three abandoned Ford transits lay buried in coarse bushes and an electricity pylon was smothered with creeping ivy.

He couldn't help but feel that he was crossing a post-apocalyptic landscape, but the analogy unnerved him; perhaps this was some kind of portent.

Get with the programme, Deano, his sister snapped. *Enquiring minds do not wander off piste. Get the story then go and nurse the prospect of Armageddon. Leave that shit for the pessimists.*

He shook her off and weaved through the abandoned vehicles and storage palettes. A hangar door loomed, and he craned his neck to look at the apex. An impressive height yet locked shut by two huge padlocks with links as thick as his arm.

He followed the building's perimeter and, after a quarter mile of factory wall, came to a corner. He turned and saw the unit stretched away from him for a considerable distance. But this time its uniformity was broken by a covered entrance accessed by a short run of steps.

A reception area.

It took him five minutes before he was close enough to confirm his suspicions. The porch had a fading RED Co. banner and a set of entrance doors made of glass and wood. One of these was ajar and the pane had been smashed.

He walked up the steps and peered through the gap in the door. Beyond the pool of light afforded by the doorway, it was dark and he fumbled for the pen torch on his key ring. The meagre torch beam uncovered a modest reception suite and, to Dean's surprise, it was still fully furnished. He opened the door to allow in more light.

Chairs and coffee tables languished under plastic sheets that shivered as he passed. The reception desk was long and strewn with tangled wires, redundant now the equipment they serviced had gone. Removed when the plant had closed, or stolen since, was a question that Dean courted for a few seconds but then he saw the sign marked Executive Suite—First Floor and this took precedent.

He found a stairwell and opened the access door. He was startled when wall-mounted lights sputtered into life and the space was splashed with a dull, creamy hue. Dean had misgivings, given the plant clearly still had limited power to keep motion sensors and emergency lighting active. Yet, outside, the place had gone to shit.

With his footfalls echoing about him, he climbed the stairs to the first floor. There, in the twilight of emergency lighting, he found three offices. Part of him, the suspicious journalist, wasn't surprised to find every door locked. He looked at the small brass plaque on each and opted for one marked Executive Director of Operations.

He kicked open the door with two hefty blows, pausing only to make sure his activities—his criminal activities—hadn't drawn any attention.

Once inside, he closed the battered door behind him.

* * *

To the ill-informed it would have appeared as though Dean uncovered the files by pure chance.

He'd gone to the desk, a large and ornate piece made from rosewood but dulled by dust. He tried the drawers which opened smoothly and found them to be empty, save for a few sheets of production data.

Empty drawers stoked the investigative journalist, a creature that was all too familiar with the concept of hiding things in plain sight. He'd come across many examples of it, ruses that tested overstretched, and poorly resourced, government officials. A drawer would only be a drawer, either with or without contents—contents that may have been pulled during the investigation following the food scandal. It didn't matter at that point in time but Dean knew drawers of executives of large conglomerates tended to house secrets. A photograph of a mistress or a bastard child, the calling card of a hooker, lists of illicit business dealings—he'd come across them all in his time. He had a theory that people in positions of power stored secrets the same way a serial killer hoarded the trophies of his victims. Perhaps they got off on it, knowing such things were there, close to them, the thrill of knowing, of being found out, adding to their sense of arrogance and superiority over others.

The hidden compartment was in the third drawer. And inside it was a slim, black USB flash drive. Dean pocketed it and left the office, his heart thumping with the familiar excitement he experienced each time he'd sniffed out a lead.

He left the plant and fought his way back through the fence, keen to dig out his laptop and unlock some dirt on RED Co. Only one thing kept him from allowing his excitement to consume him, and that was the feeling that he was being watched.

* * *

Dean's only reservation, that the flash drive was encrypted, proved unfounded as his laptop splashed the device's contents across the screen.

In his Audi, computer propped between his lap and the steering wheel, Dean took a swig of Ol' Jim from his silver flask. He scanned the data. The flash drive contained a single file, the diary of one Derek Rathbone—executive director of operations for RED Co.—who was expressing concerns with regards to the properties of their GM food programme.

Dean was intrigued by entries denoting a series of meetings Rathbone attended a year before the scandal as he re-read it to try and clarify its properties.

'Professor Green insisted on a meeting this evening. He may be a genius in his field but the man is infernal and, dare I say it, a little unhinged?

It appears that he has a proposal, a means to extend the programme beyond the parameters of the initial action plan. I am intrigued, albeit a little irritated, by his insistence to meet.'

Another entry read:

'I am now convinced that Green is truly insane. I can understand his motivations, I am a father too, but what he is suggesting is not only controversial but highly illegal. The intention, to introduce pharmaceutical prophylactic compounds to our products in order to pre-empt disease, is a remarkable if ill-conceived premise.

Yet, despite this, I can only see the kind of innovation not seen since H. Trendley Dean and his inspired view to add fluoride to the Michigan water supply and its impact on reducing cavities. RED Co. may be the pioneer in corporate-driven public health initiatives and recoup the market share this will afford. I shall take this to the board as a tentative proposal.'

Dean moved on to another entry.

'The board can see the value of Green's proposal, though I have, of course, claimed the concept as my own. A project team is to be convened and Green shall be chair. Research into Sample 10, as the compound is now known, will begin with immediate effect.

It is good to know that the board are being prospective and making inroads with our supporters in the house. There appears to be little resistance to the idea of a small-scale study. Green has chosen his disease. It is rare and therefore below the radar. We shall begin the programme within a five week window.'

'Oh, man,' Dean whispered. 'The food wasn't contaminated at all. You guys were adding stuff to it. And someone in the government knew about it, sanctioned it?'

This was huge, no, beyond huge. But it explained why RED Co. had been fined and some of their small fry staff imprisoned. Someone didn't want the boat rocked in case it capsized in the potential political storm.

He continued reading.

'Things have become untenable. Green has discussed his findings and it would appear all is not as it first seemed. The supplement we have added appears to cause the compound to destabilise over a six-week period. To the consumer there is no discernible difference, but on a genetic level there is what can only be described as mutation. To what extent Green cannot say but we must suspend production. I have asked him to provide a prospective model and from this we shall review our options.'

Rathbone's next entry began to put Dean into familiar territory. It was one of exasperation, the ramblings of someone who was floundering to find reason in an act of madness.

'I am without words! Despite Green's model stating implicitly that genetic mutation will occur in any individual who consumes products containing Sample 10, the errant professor has allowed further products into the marketplace. We cannot be sure what products contain the compound or how many units are in the food chain. I have a contingency, but there is no guarantee a product recall will secure every unit sold.

I have sent for Green but his staff have not seen him since word of his misdemeanour became known. The professor's concern for his daughter's well-being has put potentially thousands at risk. Yet this is but a conservative estimate. If Sample 10 should contaminate the gene pool then Lord knows what the implications may be for mankind.'

The last entry pretty much summed up what Dean already knew, though it did clarify that any leak about RED Co. and GM produce had been contrived as part of Rathbone's contingency. Green was a wanted man, and not all parties were that concerned in what condition he was found.

The truth was the professor appeared to have disappeared as though he'd never existed in the first place. Dean had a terrible sense of familiarity whenever he heard the name Professor Green, as though he really should know the guy, but he shelved it.

His stomach rumbled and he realised he'd skipped lunch so that he could appease Cound by driving down to Wellington. He'd made a decision to go to the town and find lodgings for the night the moment an articulated truck rumbled past. He looked up and recognised it immediately as one of those belonging to RED Co. and it had come from the direction of the town.

In an instant, Dean lost his appetite, but headed into town anyway. In times like these comfort came as a liquid, and he intended to bathe for a long time.

* * *

The town of Wellington was over three hundred years old. In its time it had been witness to many events, a civil war (Cromwell was rumoured to have had a stronghold there) and two World Wars in which more than two hundred of its young men had perished.

Dean drove into the town centre where the cenotaph to the town's dead stood on a plinth like a sentinel protecting their memory, and the mishmash of black-and-white timbered buildings and thatched cottages gave the square a sedate air that only came with a rural setting.

That was until he saw the ambulance.

It sped past him, seemingly coming from nowhere, its flasher unit splashing the buildings with intermittent blue light. The siren whooped once and the vehicle pulled up outside a small pub that claimed to be The Pheasant.

Dean spotted the parking bays lined up outside the building and took note of the patrons' only sign. He parked, climbed out of his car and took his laptop case with him as a small crowd gathered outside the pub.

The ambulance crew climbed from the cab, their green coveralls in stark contrast to the building's cream wall. One of the paramedics, a small woman with severely short blonde hair, called to the crowd. 'Where's the casualty?'

'Inside,' said a portly middle-aged man with a bushy grey moustache and eyebrows to match. 'There's something strange going on with him.'

'Is he conscious?' This came from the other paramedic, a tall man with the kind of chest that could bench press two hundred pounds. He towered over his female colleague.

'Conscious?' the man with the moustache repeated. 'Yeah, he's pretty active too. We've already called the police.'

Despite his size, the tall paramedic stalled. 'Police? Is the casualty violent?'

'He's had a go at a few of us,' the man said.

'In what way?' the woman asked.

'Tried to bite us,' Mr Moustache explained. 'Just went mad. I've known old Charlie Boswell for years and he ain't got a bad bone in his body. But tonight he just went crazy.'

'Tell 'em about his eyes, Henry,' said a rotund woman standing next to Mr Moustache.

'Yes, Henry,' the female paramedic said. 'Tell us about Mr Boswell's eyes.'

'Never seen anything like it,' the woman pressed. 'As yellow as the sun they are. Can you believe it?'

Dean merged with the crowd. No one paid him any mind; events were making him invisible.

'So where is Mr Boswell now?' The male paramedic was fidgeting on the spot. Anxiety liked attention; he'd learned that a while ago.

'Tommy Pledger and his lad are with him.' Henry nodded to the male paramedic. 'Those guys are built like you, fella. And Charlie has twenty years on 'em, but he's given 'em a run for their money.'

'We need to wait for the police,' the female paramedic said. 'It's protocol.'

Before anyone could question this, a loud cry came from inside the pub. It was followed by a crash and the sound of breaking glass.

'He's loose!' The shout was shrill and laced with fear. The door to the pub was filled by a young, heavy-set man with a shaved head. He had a wild look in his eyes, like a terrified horse running from a burning stable. His denim shirt was splashed with dark blood and he leapt down the steps as though they weren't there at all, knocking the male paramedic aside.

A screech of car tyres added to the commotion. A police car skidded to a halt twenty yards away. The vehicle rocked as two burly officers emerged in unison and made for the crowd.

The group shied away, the tide of bodies sweeping Dean along with it. He fought his way through, his inquisitiveness forever an insatiable beast, getting to the front row just as the doors to the pub crashed open, inciting a gasp from those about him.

On the steps stood an elderly man, his stooped posture reminding Dean of an ape. Henry hadn't been exaggerating; Boswell's eyes were bright yellow, and the man's aged face was pulled into an animalistic sneer.

Without hesitation the police officers drew their batons.

'Stay where you are, sir,' one of them said to Boswell. 'You're sick and in need of medical attention.'

The expression on the female paramedic's face said, *he sure does but I ain't got a fucking clue as to what's wrong with him and how to treat it.*

Boswell merely snarled. He bared his bloodied teeth but they were bizarrely askew and Dean realised the guy was wearing dentures. Boswell launched himself from the steps. He hit the officer squarely in the chest and both went sprawling.

The second officer stepped up and struck Boswell once on the shoulder and the street was filled with the sickening pop of a clavicle shattering. Under normal circumstances such a blow would have ended the assault.

But Boswell continued to try and maul the officer beneath him, his head thrashing to get to his victim.

'Jesus, Bill,' the officer gasped. 'Hit him again! The fucker's goin' for my throat!'

Police officer Bill drew back his arm and swept the baton in a wide arc so it made contact with Boswell's head. High-carbon steel met the bone of the old man's skull and the force of it took him sideways and ejected his dentures across the square where they clattered into a storm drain.

This time Boswell lay still, save for one of his hands which went into spasm, making his watch click on the kerb.

The floored police officer got to his feet, his expression indicating that he was trying to make sense of what had just happened.

'You okay, Al?' police officer Bill asked his colleague.

'Yeah,' police officer Al replied, though his fear wasn't prepared to take a hike just yet.

'Now what?' the male paramedic asked.

Police officer Al's gaze remained on Boswell's crumpled body.

'Now you get this thing in the back of your unit and take it to someone who knows what the hell it might be,' he said.

'It's a human being,' the female paramedic said with contempt directed at Al.

No one said anything. Dean suspected that, like him, no one in the crowd could really be certain enough to agree with her.

* * *

'I'm surprised you want to stay,' Henry said as he ran Dean's credit card through the ATM unit on the bar. 'I mean, having a copper floored by a patron on your doorstep isn't the best advertisement for a pub.'

Dean smiled. 'I've been in some pubs where that's part of the criteria for admission, if you get my meaning?'

Henry chuckled and went to the hand pumps. 'One from me on the house as a thank you for not pissing off down to The Three Feathers?'

'You mean there's another pub around here?' Dean pulled a mock surprised face.

'Comedian, eh?' Henry said with a grin. 'You'll fit in around here. What can I get you?'

'Lager, please.'

'City boy?' Henry asked.

Dean nodded. 'How'd you guess?'

'Locals like local ale,' Henry explained, handing him the beer.

'The guy who went apeshit,' Dean said, 'was he a local?'

'Known Charlie forever,' the landlord said.

'So, what happened?'

'It's like I told the police, Charlie is as soft as shite. I've never seen him like that, ever,' said Henry. 'One minute he's sat where you are now, talking about the last food drop. And the next he's creating havoc in my bar.'

'Food drop?' Dean said after taking a sip from his pint.

'We've got the same problems as everywhere else at the moment, fella,' Henry said. 'And some folk are having to use the same solution.'

'RED Co.?'

'Yeah,' Henry said.

'I guess you guys have more affinity with them than most,' Dean said. 'On account of the plant?'

'A boon and a curse in the same pot,' Henry said. 'Wellington lost more than RED Co. when the plant closed. It's taken a while for the local economy to pick up. I guess they feel they owe us.'

'So you get a regular food drop?' Dean said.

'Not regular, but prioritised. I mean, we got one of the first. And now they're back today.'

The moment became pensive and both men took the time to savour it.

'Anyway,' Henry said, clapping his hands together. 'At least the food drop means I can still provide a menu. What would you like?'

Dean considered Sample 10 and Green's wayward experiment. He thought about food given away by RED Co. and the potential implications.

'Think I'll just have a few bag of those pork scratchings,' Dean said as he hid behind his beer.

'You know these things will kill you, right?' Henry said reaching for the packets secured in their display tray.

Dean chuckled at the irony of the barman's statement.

* * *

The compound is alive with activity. There is an excitement that Dean has not felt for some time. It's been a while since the containment cell was home but even with the new-found freedom of the base, it still feels like a prison.

Same people, same faces, same routines. Get up in the morning; take the pills dispensed from a compartmentalised plastic tray, brought by a smiling lady with a name badge that says her name is Monica. Then it is into the labs to be wired to a battery of machines that whirr and bleep as the treadmill cranks up. After this, blood samples are taken and lunchtime is spent in the mess hall, eating alone, served by suited figures with the ever-present biochem masks.

The afternoons are a mix of reading text books and TV. Then dinner is served in the small apartment that has become home over a period of time now indeterminate. Life is routine, no room for the random, orchestrated by time tables and progress charts.

Sometimes, as the TV talks of places in other parts of the world, the urge to leave the base swamps him. Then the guilt comes, beating down the wanderlust, making him feel ungrateful for a life dedicated to keeping him alive. Keeping him safe.

The outside is never too far away. The arrival of the trucks is an example of this. They lumber into the compound, twelve sixteen-wheeler trucks with RED Co. on their tarpaulin skin. The trucks park up side by side, two rows of six, metal haloed by tall floodlights pouring iridescence onto the compound.

An evening run has led him here. Again, part of a routine to keep the body fit, allow it to maintain itself at its optimum and limit the chances of illness regaining a foothold.

The noise of the trucks has drawn him here like the clichéd moth to a flame. Yet he is just as mesmerised as the trucks kill their engines and silence returns. The high walls will keep their secrets well; they always do.

As the silent vigil continues, the men who climb down from the cabs move to the back of the trucks and throw open the huge doors.

From the small, single-storey buildings scattered about the compound others emerge. Like ants, these newcomers, many recognisable from the base, join the people at the back of the trucks as boxes are unloaded. These boxes are then taken back into the base, an efficient process that is astounding to watch.

Soon the trucks are empty and the doors slammed shut. The tiny thuds of cab doors closing come slightly afterwards. Then the big engines are gunning again, almost in unison.

With a belch of diesel and the thunder of engines, the convoy moves out, the vibrations at their passing rattling the chain links on the gate. He watches them go, unable to shake a sudden feeling that this is an event he should not have witnessed. Then the rot truly sets in as part of him calls out, insistent like an alarm call, and he begins to question not just where, but who, he is.

The compound begins to fragment, as though the world is coming apart before his very eyes, a façade smashed aside by reality.

* * *

Dean's sleep was fitful and, when he finally climbed from his bed, it took twenty minutes in the shower to make him feel anywhere near human again. This made him think about Boswell and how human he was feeling at that moment.

His stomach growled, as though complaining at the enforced food ban. Dean went to the small unit that nurtured a TV and kettle where he ripped open another packet of scratchings.

He sat on his bed and flicked through the channels. They all spoke of yesterday's news as though it was current, the food distribution issues continued and RED Co. wagons featured in so many reports it may as well have been a corporate induction video.

At seven thirty Dean called Cound at the office and left a message to say he'd got his angle and would be in later to pitch it. Then he packed and went downstairs to a small booth that served as The Pheasant's B+B reception area. It was unattended and he left his key on the counter with a thank you note.

As he drove out of Wellington, the realisation that something was untoward dawned on him when he hit the motorway at rush hour and found that, instead of having to sit in three lanes of slow moving traffic, the roads were almost empty.

* * *

'Where the hell is everyone?' Dean asked Cound.

The office was as quiet as the motorway, and brought with it an eerie silence that left both feeling out of sorts. Occasionally a lone figure would walk past the pod, a secretary with a slip of papers. Dean knew her in passing but couldn't recall her name. He watched her slim frame glide by, short black skirt hugging her tight bottom. These days he took his diversions wherever they were presented. Passing strangers were a specialty of his, relationships on the hoof. There was only ever one constant and sooner or later Ol' Jim was too much of a potent lover to divorce.

'Maybe everyone's decided to adopt your work ethic, Sharp,' Cound grumbled. 'Maybe my news team is out on the mother of all benders as we speak.'

'Funny guy,' Dean said without humour.

'If I had a sense of humour I wouldn't be doing this for a living,' Cound said as his face disappeared behind his mug of coffee.

His editor's comment lacked conviction. The guy's presence was usually formidable but today he appeared lacklustre. A skeleton crew turnout didn't appear to have any impact whatsoever.

'You okay, boss?' Dean asked.

'What are you, my mother?'

'Just asking,' Dean said.

'Fuck me,' Cound said. 'My resident drunk is concerned about my welfare. The world really has gone to shit.'

'You think that?' Dean asked.

'It ain't the same as it was,' Cound said. 'Anyone with eyes can see that.'

'You think my pitch has anything to do with it?' Dean asked.

'Your pitch is one among many theories being pumped out by Reuters, Sharp,' Cound said. 'RED Co. is trying to put a Band Aid on their bad.'

'So you think that's what this is, a PR stunt?' Dean shifted in his chair. It wasn't like Cound to be so conservative. 'The food drops may contain items that have been contaminated by Sample 10.'

'Food drops are giving people hope. Running a story that removes that at the moment will cost us readers and cause panic,' Cound countered.

'So what does that mean?' Dean said.

'It means that you do more homework,' Cound said. 'You go and find someone to corroborate your story. What about Rathbone?'

'You think an executive director of operations directly responsible for illegal drug testing is going to talk to me about his involvement?'

'You need to find someone, Sharp,' Cound said, his tone brisk. 'I will not be held responsible for panic in the streets, you got that? The government already has cross hairs on the press after the Levinson Inquiry. I'm not sticking my head out of the trench until you give me hard proof, an interview, on record, with someone involved, at least.'

'For fuck's sake,' Dean said as he stood to leave Cound's office. 'I'm getting out of here.'

'Where are you going?' Cound snapped.

'I'm off to see the mother of all benders, boss,' Dean said. 'Maybe she'll give me some appreciation.'

Cound made several threats as Dean walked away but at that point in time they meant nothing. He'd revisit them later, when he'd spent a few days in the company of Ol' Jim and the blissful oblivion it so often brought.

He wished for the world to change while he was away. That things would be back to normal.

Sadly, when he did come round in his flat twenty-four hours later, only his first wish had been granted.

FIGHTING TO SURVIVE

The trucks are back. It barely seems a moment since their greasy departure from the compound. This is the nature of a contrived life in a clinical world; time becomes meaningless, one day blurring into the next, months and years are shapeless entities, without substance.

Time really does go on, the physical changes he feels proof positive of such a tenet. No longer weak and unsure entities, confidence is now as familiar as the trucks that pull into the compound, great beasts of tarpaulin and metal, heaving their oily smoke into the air.

The exchange is a reverse of their last visit. Boxes are brought out from the buildings and placed inside the trucks that wait, doors hanging wide, and the beasts are fed until their innards are bursting.

As they leave for a final time, Dean watches from the shadows. This will need to be kept secret, he feels this with total certainty, the conviction holding him still, making him a statue in the dark.

The trucks rumble away. But doubt arrives. He knows many things in this life, but somehow part of him feels as though he isn't meant to, that his presence here is imposition on a grand scale.

He cannot help but feel that he is seeing things of such importance yet he remains detached, as though peering at a scene through a sheet of Perspex.

The next thing he knows is that he is awake and any contention he held only moments ago has been forgotten, lost to a fading dreamscape without reference point or contour.

* * *

Dean blinked several times. He'd winked out for a while and wasn't surprised, given his recent experiences with the deranged traffic warden. Shame that the hip flask was empty, but the streets beyond the foyer door were not. His would-be nemesis had mutated again and was now a bloated pink and purple humanoid, skin corrugated by the restrictions of her tattered uniform, eyes as black as a Nazi's heart. Far from giving out tickets, the bitch just wanted to rip out his throat. She lathered her bloated tongue against the pane as though trying to savour him through the glass. He peered back at her, his body taut, and moist sweat seeping through his blood-streaked cotton shirt. As her frenzied gaze fell upon him, he realised he'd become a cannibal's wet dream.

Dean's thoughts were an incomprehensible blend of fear and hopelessness. He needed some inspiration, and fast. Any decision needed to be based on available options and these were limited, if not non-existent.

There are always options, Deano, Jenna sneered. *It's just that you never had the balls to take them. Not the real ones. Not the ones that mattered.*

He shook his head, partly to be free of her taunts, partly in disagreement. His malignant psyche had dislodged something, though, he was thinking again, and this placed him in a better position than succumbing to despair.

He couldn't go back to his flat. Those things were abroad and he risked running into them. He couldn't stay in the foyer. Sooner or later he'd need Ol' Jim and become reckless in his haste to quell the taste.

'If I can't go up I have to go down,' he said, his gaze flitting to Annison's body.

Dean stood but introduced a stoop to try to avoid the black, hungry stare from the warden. Eager, slapping sounds against the door told him he hadn't quite pulled it off.

He climbed over the counter, doing his best to avoid the pool of congealed blood that lapped against the base of a telephone. Behind the reception area lay an office, a staff toilet and the target of his search; the door to the basement. The white paintwork had a sign on it that said the entrance was for authorised personnel only. Given that there were few still alive to give him authority, Dean decided to take the notice under advisement. He turned the handle and opened the door. A long flight of steps, lit by stark fluorescents, plunged into the bowels of the building. Despite his predicament, Dean needed to fire up his resolve to get himself onto the steps.

He made the descent, trailing his fingers lightly on the handrail bolted to the wall on his right. Every few steps he would pause and listen out for telltale signs that he had company.

What the hell are you doing, Deano? Jenna was ever the irritant in times of doubt. *You're hoping to find a way out by boxing yourself in? Anything could be waiting for you down there.*

But he knew there would be a way out, a service entrance for maintenance staff, most likely, a place where soiled work boots wouldn't leave dirty marks on pristine linoleum.

So he pressed on until he reached the bottom. His world was gradually filled with the heavy throb of machinery and the heady smell of diesel and cleaning fluids.

Overhead, rows of thick pipes, conduits that provided utilities to the building above, stretched out before him. Nearby, the pounding pulse of a huge generator made him eager to move on, his ears finding the sound far more irritating than his sister's moaning.

Footfalls echoed as he followed the corridor, and at intervals he came across doors or inlets that held either cleaning or maintenance products. In one, he found a toolbox and dug out a claw hammer. He felt its weight and had a few practice swings before deciding it was going to keep him company in his quest for an exit.

The corridor reflected the size of the building. Dean had followed the passageway for ten minutes when, finally, it became an open square with several huge pipes rising from the floor. This network went left in a series of U-bends and the metal, painted deep crimson, was slick with moisture.

Dean walked into the open. The snarl came immediately and from the deep shadows, something charged at him.

The thing wore the overalls of a maintenance worker. There, any similarity to a human being ended, save for the bloated appendages that served for arms and legs. There were eyes of a sort, sunken and chasm-black, and these were fixed onto him, their lack of emotion as chilling as its intention to rip him apart.

Dean backed away, towards the passage; his plan was to get into a closed space so that the thing had less opportunity to flank him. However, his feet got tangled and failed him, and he fell backwards with a shout of frustration. At this point luck stayed on his side. The creature pounced seconds before Dean fell, and it sailed overhead as it tried to strike down the spot in the air where he'd been only moments ago.

There was a heavy thud as soft tissue hit firm concrete and a long, mournful howl filled the pump room. Dean scrambled to his feet, the hammer ready, in time to see the creature struggling to stand, its head even more misshapen than a few moments before.

Yet the beast still made an attempt to get to him and Dean felt fear boil until it became anger. He ran at the fallen creature and began pounding it with the hammer. The blows were wild to begin with, the hammer head sinking into flesh, removing wads that slapped against the walls and floor.

His assault became concentrated, the thing's head now the focus, the terrible sounds of cracking and popping were distant entities, and he was shocked to find that the loud, feral growls and snarls were no longer coming from the creature, they were coming from him as the savage attack became a cathartic vehicle in which his fear pumped the gas.

The head came apart and the contents rolled out like an ocean viewed in slow motion. As the grey matter hit the air, it steamed like hot porridge in a cold kitchen.

Dean fell to his knees and vomited, his sides pumping until they ached. Was this the New World Order, man having to become a

Barbarian in order to survive? He didn't know if he could do it, if he cared enough to do it. God, he needed a slug of Ol' Jim.

No, Deano, you need to get out of that pump room and then the city. Fight for something, for once in your life, fight to stay alive.

'What's the point?' he asked the corpse next to him. 'What good would it do even if I manage to find a place to hole up?'

Maybe you could think positive? Maybe this isn't happening everywhere and help will come? Ever thought of that, Deano?

Jenna was right. No, not Jenna, never Jenna, him and him alone. Doubt and scorn may have had Jenna's voice but they belonged to him. His sister wasn't here, couldn't be depended on. Hell, for all he knew she may have had her head buried into some hapless soul's stomach, her jaws opening and closing like an elevator door in overdrive.

Dean wiped snot and puke onto the sleeve of his coat and got to his feet. The hammer was heavy in his hand and he looked down at it. He held the tool up to his face and stared at the remnants of skull and cranial matter coating its stainless steel surface. This was his saviour, his instrument of destruction, and its injunction would be testament to his resolve, his hope, that whatever was happening within the city did not extend outside its bloodied walls.

On his knees he stared at the pipe work, the distant thrum of the air conditioning keeping a time with the beat of his heart. His mind wanted out for a while. It needed to seek out a place where it could take stock and rally its strength.

For the sake of his own sanity, he made no attempt to stop it.

* * *

The walls are streaked with blood. It traverses the magnolia paintwork like crimson tears on sallow cheeks. These very corridors have been a place of relentless routine for so long it is difficult to comprehend the changes taking place. There is one constant: he is running. Just as his fitness regimen would have him passing through these corridors at speed, so he runs now. But this is not exercise, this is all about survival. The detail is sketchy but the images about him are vivid enough.

The figures in the white suits are now splashed red, limbs severed, bodies defiled by an enemy that knows no mercy. The staff run ahead of him, screams and shouts muzzled by the biochem masks. There is an unsettling feeling in his chest, a surge of fluttering excitement, anxiety massaging his heart.

The world winks out, the figures disappear, then the corridor returns, time playing with his mind as the exit lies ahead, the people in front of him are now gone, but fresh screams come from behind him, wails that seem to go on forever.

The blackness returns, and when it decamps, he is now outside in the compound. The staff there a r e ripped open, their bodies steaming in the cold air.

There are sounds from all about him, snarls and barks that carry across the space, filling every corner, as does the blood. The gate is ahead, barring any means of escape. On the ground lies the ruined remains of the woman he knows as Monica. He does not recognise her; the ravaged hole that sits in her face doesn't allow for that, instead her badge gives her identity away.

A flustered moment comes as hands search for a pass in Monica's bloodied clothing. The air is full of the stink of shit and vomit; intestines loll to one side like ropes on a quayside. Finally, after what seems like a lifetime, trembling fingers clutch at a laminated ID card. Monica's image smiles up at him through a mist of gore from a face that is gone.

He heads to the swipe slot on the gate. It is bulky and grey and contains two plastic blisters on its apex. On the box, the blister on the left begins to glow bright red. Dean uses his jeans to rub tacky blood away from the card. He locates the magnetic strip, and for a second steals a dead woman's identity. The box on the gate buzzes like a bad quiz show klaxon. The plastic blisters become united as both turn green. There is a huge sound of metal being moved against concrete and the barrier slides on casters that have worn a groove in the concrete yard it protects from the outside world.

He doesn't wait for it to finish its journey; in fact the gate has barely begun to move before he squeezes himself through the opening. Then he is free, running headlong and trying to ignore the moans of the dying. After a while the wind whips these away and he stops, doubled over. He vomits onto rich green grass that undulates under the caress of the breeze.

He looks up at the horizon and considers his next move. No sooner has he focused on this he knows what he has to do. It comes to him like an instinct, a calling from afar.

Like a hound tracking the scent of a wily fox he continues to run, making his way north.

To the city.

* * *

In the depths of his apartment building, Dean came across the exit ten minutes later. It was a fire door with a horizontal steel bar which had to be depressed in order for him to pass.

As he went through, there was a wall facing him, and a heavily fashioned iron gate. He looked left and noted a short path that culminated in a door marked as maintenance locker.

His pessimistic mind tried to grab his attention by yelling; he'd almost got himself killed for a dead end. It was a brief parley. Dean tested the gate and found that it gave way when he pushed it.

Rather than go back, Dean decided to take his chances and go through the gate. The hinges creaked as he went and, at another time, in another life, he would have made some glib comment about what the annual service charge was actually for, but not today. Today was not about the trivia of a comfortable life, it was about not ending up dead.

Beyond the gate was an open stretch of land comprising twin lawns, both edged by tall acacia trees and an ornate, half-height wall with spiked railings surrounding the greenery. A shale path separated the lawns and ended in a security gate.

As the wind passed through their branches, the trees hissed like coiled snakes ready to strike. Yet, as unsettling as this seemed, Dean was too concerned with the commotion coming from the city to pay it anything more than token attention.

There was screaming—lots of it.

It came in on air tinged with smoke and the hideous reek of rotten meat. Dean gagged and remembered his 'breathe through the mouth' mantra. As he followed the path, he noted the lawns were immaculate, but here and there pools of deep crimson marred the effect. He passed a sign that asked those in a world that cared about such things not to walk on the grass.

But it's okay to bleed on there, Dean thought without mirth. *No choice in this realm of chaos.*

He reached the security gate and looked out, gripping a vertical bar with one hand like a prisoner longing for freedom. A small car park lay ahead. It belonged to a building opposite, a tall glass structure that was streaming smoke from the top floor. All the cars were either burnt out or trashed, as though a breakers yard had landed overnight.

He rested his head against the cool metal.

'Now what?' he said. It was rhetoric, no resolution currently in the back pocket. But even if he'd had an answer lined up ready he would never have had chance to voice it.

Because an army of snarling salivating creatures started dropping onto the lawns.

* * *

Incredulously, Dean watched them land. At first he didn't understand how it could be happening but when he looked back at his building, he noticed the windows and stepped back in horror, the gate reminding him he was out of places to go.

Each window pane was crammed with twisted faces, multiple limbs punching out the glass. Some windows were already broken and creatures, like those he'd just seen landing on the lawn, were leaping through, regardless of their own safety.

What he was seeing was as incomprehensible as anything he'd seen that morning. His block had turned. Every man, woman and child was now a vicious, malformed creature needing to kill, to feed.

They came at him, for him, and he fumbled with the gate in an urgent attempt to get out. His tranquil respite was fast becoming his prison and he managed to squeeze through shortly before the first beast could reach for him.

He slammed the gate and ran, unclear as to how close the metamorphic tenants were in pursuit. Nor did he know what lay ahead. The car park appeared devoid of any life form, human or not, and he crossed it quickly, heading for the city streets.

The car park led to a small exit ramp that went downwards as it disappeared into a covered archway. Dean was no longer in a position to hesitate, the squeal of metal letting him know the iron gate that had bought him some time was being wrenched off of its hinges. Soon a deadly, hungry flood of creatures would be flowing through the car park.

The exit tunnel received him, and inside it was cool and reeked of dampness, but he drew some comfort from it for mere seconds. Ahead the world was captured in an archway. Before him rows of shops, three storeys high, and red and green awnings threw rectangular shadows onto the pavement.

Dean continued running. Others did the same, people screaming as they went; some clutching at their limbs where deep, brutal wounds poured blood. Across the road, one man was driven through the plate glass window of a bakery; a massive shard of glass fell and removed his legs at the thigh. Creatures were on him before he had time to scream. Stumps rose from the melee as the savagery threw the man onto his back and twin plumes of blood lifted skyward like paint in a high-budget commercial.

Dean peeled left, now out in the open, hoping to get lost in the chaos. Creatures were everywhere he looked. Dean zigzagged through the cramped streets, the pavement littered with disfigured bodies and debris pulled from the fractured shops.

A young woman was sat on the kerb; she rocked and cradled a bloody swatch of linen in her arms. A small ruined arm hung limply from the material. Dean was almost upon her as she leaned forwards and took a bite out of the limb. Horrified, he pulled up and his presence had her snapping her head around to face him, yellow eyes glowing beneath eyebrows carved into a V.

Dean swerved to avoid her, moving at speed to put distance between him and the awful sight. At once she lost interest in him, and the young mutant mother returned to enjoying quality time with her baby.

* * *

Dean's thoughts of survival were diminishing fast. In fact, he was beginning to think that clinging to them was dangerously close to delusional. And who could blame him given the ghastly events he'd witnessed?

There were just too many of them, cleaving through the local population the way locusts ravaged crops. People didn't stand a chance, struck down and savaged where they fell.

Dean guessed it was only a matter of time until his luck went south. Sooner or later, the crowds would thin as the dead outnumbered the living. Hiding would be more difficult. He had to get off of the streets, and fast.

Panic was always trying to claim him, but he battled it, with as much vigour as he fought the creatures about him. He raced past stores, most of them broken or ablaze, and circumvented a telephone box when it became apparent its occupant was reshaping into one of the creatures, receiver still in hand.

Then he saw the church. It was set back from the road, kept separate by a graveyard with many grey tombstones. Dean went to it, consumed by the overpowering sense that it was the right thing to do. The faithful would have considered it an epiphany, though Dean would think it merely the most obvious choice given its thick stone walls and limited points of access.

He charged, shoulders low, his lungs hot with exertion. To his dismay a group of creatures smashed their way out of a store and onto the street, and in their newly fashioned egress barred his way.

He pulled up and they became aware of him. Dean lifted the hammer and it felt pitifully inadequate for the occasion.

With a cacophony of savage cries, they came at him. And he braced for the inevitable agony.

* * *

The agony never came. What came instead was the roar of gunfire from behind the creatures, a sleek plane screaming low, nose cone spitting white fire down from the heavens.

Dean dived into a doorway as the street exploded under the onslaught of a high-calibre machine gun. Creatures stood snarling at the sky shortly before their bloated bodies were shredded. Many lost limbs yet their fury remained. A multitude of beasts screamed animalistic curses into the sky as streaks of white light cut them down. Chunks of brick and concrete were blasted into the street where it became deadly shrapnel, carving flesh and shattering bone.

The jet roared away, leaving the scene coated in smoke and dust.

Disorientated, Dean climbed from his hiding place, his throat bitter with the taste of brick dust.

Hands were about him and he began to fight against them, the hammer raised, poised to break skulls before anything could clamp its jaws on him.

A woman stood before him, black hair turned grey with dust, her eyes yellow orbs. He almost brought the hammer down when she did something to stop him.

She said his name.

* * *

'What the fuck?' It was about as articulate as his brain would allow. Given the circumstances he thought he'd done pretty well to say anything at all.

'Come with me, Dean,' she said. 'To the church.'

'I don't even know who you are,' he said. 'And what the fuck's wrong with your eyes?'

'I'll tell you,' she said. 'In the church.'

'You could be ripping out my throat in the church,' he said.

'I'm not one of them,' the woman said. 'I'm not contaminated.'

'What do you know about contamination?' His paranoia was as wild as the beasts marauding through the city.

'I'll tell you everything—' She stopped.

'In the church, right?' he pre-empted.

She nodded; her pale face pathetically beautiful despite smears of dirt.

'Fuck it,' he said. 'Who cares where you kill me, right? Lead the way.'

* * *

They weaved their way through the carnage. The aircraft's run had been indiscriminate, the act of desperation, containment, leaving human and inhuman bodies to lie together, brutalised and bleeding, like some macabre sculpture.

The woman was by his side, and Dean tried desperately to avoid her gaze. Even the shocking images about him seemed preferable. She seemed to understand his discomfort and pulled a small case from the pocket of her short, red jacket. Within moments she'd cracked it open and slid sunglasses onto the bridge of her small, upturned nose.

'Sorry,' she said. 'I forget they unsettle people.'

Dean said nothing. He looked at the church where a red board sported gold letters that gave the building an identity.

St Bartholomew's, RC Church.

He tried to ignore the bloody hand print on the banner. They passed through tall, wrought iron gates, stepping over the bodies of several creatures culled in the aerial assault.

The church rose before them, a majestic reverent structure climbing from a world of barbarism. The stone was dark and lichen grew in patches of shocking green.

'Seems appropriate to seek refuge in the kind of place noted for sanctuary,' the woman said.

'You saying the world is lost?' Dean asked.

'I'm saying the world is different,' she replied as she pushed open the large doors. 'And we need a place to figure out just how much it's changed.'

'How we can get it back?' Dean offered.

'If we can get it back,' she said.

They walked into the church and shut the doors behind them.

* * *

'So what happened to you?' Dean asked the woman as he sat in a pew. The church smelled of candle wax and old wood. High in the ceiling a fashioned piece of ironwork held several electric bulbs, the only evidence that the building existed in the twenty-first century.

'You mean you don't remember the police cell?' she said. 'I was younger then.' She became coy, almost childlike, and Dean looked at her as though for the first time. Beneath her red jacket, a pale summer dress was frayed at the hem, and blue deck shoes seemed as much out of place as the uneasy smile on her lips. For a split second, the world shimmied. An overwhelming sense of déjà vu shook him awake and he fumbled for images to support this sudden notion that he'd somehow, somewhere, met this woman before. But his brain rejected any attempts to focus and his evidence slipped away. Yet it did not erase the feelings. They just sank below the surface and peered through, like a drowning face bumps against the ice of a frozen lake.

'I have a feeling we've met,' he said with a sigh. 'But that's all it is. There's no detail.'

'That would be the BW,' she said nodding as though it were obvious to all but him.

'BW?'

'Yes,' she replied. 'Brain wipe. It's a tool that my father uses to keep his dirty secrets.'

'Your father?' Dean was struggling to follow her train of thought.

'Yes, Professor Green.'

'And who is Professor Green?' Dean asked blankly. He felt as though he should know this name, too.

The woman nodded as though she understood much of what Dean did not.

'The brain wipe is one of my father's many remarkable achievements,' she said. 'Targeting specific elements of recall, like Alzheimer's disease. You can, in effect, remove the memory of specific people, specific experiences, from a person. It was taken from you and its effects are residual. You'll remember names but without context. It will be as though you are learning about them for the first time, every time they are mentioned.'

'You saying someone has fucked with my mind?' Dean's anger fizzed inside. He felt violated, tampered with, like some vivisectionist's lab animal.

'Yes,' she said simply. 'My father.'

'So how do I get to know what the fuck you're talking about?' he spat. She flinched, but he ignored it.

'I can offer you something to arrest the effects,' she said. She went to another pocket and pulled out a slim black flask.

'Unless that's booze I'm not interested,' he said.

'Then I cannot tell you what is happening,' she said flatly. 'You won't remember it tomorrow. The brain wipe won't let you.'

'I can live without knowing,' he said. He turned away. It was an act of a sulking child because he knew he couldn't live without knowing. He couldn't do that because not knowing killed him, not knowing might well kill him in this newly evolved world of carnage.

The silence played out and he used it to come to terms with the inevitable.

'Give me the flask,' he said without looking at her.

'You'll need to sit down,' she advised. 'It'll make you drowsy.'

He went to a pew and slumped into it. She came to him, her lithe figure passing in front of stained glass window where the light passed through her thin cotton dress, and her body was outlined against the material.

'What's in here?' he asked as he took the flask, popped the lid and sniffed the contents.

'An enzyme that will regenerate the areas of tissue neutralised by the brain wipe,' she explained.

'You mean I'll remember the past? How we met?'

'No,' she said. 'You just won't forget what I tell you about it all from this point on.'

'This isn't a co-incidence is it?' he said.

'What do you mean?' she replied slowly.

'You being here,' he said.

'Drink the enzyme, Dean,' she said. 'Then I can tell you everything.'

He sank the flask in three gulps and, with every swallow, wished it was Ol' Jim slipping down his throat.

* * *

She spoke and Dean listened. Her voice was soft, rhythmic as the effects of the drink worked their wonders on him. He'd gone under for a while yet he could still hear her. When he came back the questions stockpiled and he got ready to launch them.

'So your father works for RED Co.?'

'He's worked for many people,' the woman said. 'But he's his own master, make no mistake.'

The silence that followed was made sombre by the surroundings. The woman's mouth twitched at its corners. A tear emerged from the lens of her sunglasses and meandered down her cheek. She wiped it away with the back of her hand. The action smudged her cheek.

'So we've met?' he asked.

'Ten years ago, in a town called Gullcrest.' She sniffed.

'Gullcrest?' Again, the name was familiar but remained without context. 'So remind me of who you are.'

'Susan Hadley,' she said.

'Seems we're going to be here for a while, Susan,' he said, listening to the cries and snarls from outside in the besieged city. 'How about you fill in some more of those blanks for me?'

'Of course,' she said.

With that she began to hand back the memories that had been stolen from him so long ago.

* * *

'So what about you?' Dean asked when Susan stopped talking. It had taken her ten minutes to explain his lost past. 'How did you get out of the cell?'

'The men in white came for me,' she said. 'They had keys and orders to come and collect me.'

'Orders?' Dean repeated. 'From who?'

'My father, of course.' She ran a hand through her hair and the movement created a small dust cloud that danced in the sunlight coming through the window. It was an incongruent sight, a moment of beauty on the most hideous of days.

'The cell was for my own protection,' she continued. 'A place to hold me until help came.'

'Yet you ran away from the men who set you free,' Dean said. 'Why?'

'I was nine,' she said by way of explanation. 'I was scared by what they told me.'

'And what did they tell you?'

'That the town had to be destroyed to save the world.'

Dean stared at her. Despite everything that had happened up to this point, the realisation that attempts had been made to stop it staggered him.

'And how the hell did they intend to do that?' Dean whispered.

'A missile,' she said flatly. 'Loaded with incendiary. Wiped the town off of the map. We watched it, together. It was like a sunrise.'

'If the town was destroyed why is this happening today?'

'Because the science lived on,' Susan said. 'My father's work lived on. He put mankind at risk to try and save me.'

'On this scale? How?' Dean asked.

'A few days ago you were at one of their factories.' Susan held up a hand as he pulled a quizzical face. 'You were there. And so was I, watching you. You found evidence of what had been going on. Then the BW took it from you. Such is its design. Nothing could link my father to Gullcrest.'

'So what did I find?' It felt strange asking such a question. He thought he should be used to such things by now.

She told him of Wellington and what he'd found in the RED Co. plant.

'Which leads me back to the question,' he said. 'How can this be happening now if products were recalled?'

'RED Co. may have recalled the products but they weren't destroyed,' Susan said. 'My father used his influence—his ways—to secure some of it. He kept it safe. Kept it ready.'

'Ready for what?' Dean found this incredible. He wished he had a recorder or a pen and paper. As fruitless as it seemed at that point in time he felt he should be recording this for someone—anyone—to make sense of what was going on.

'Ready for a time when the memories faded. People forget the news after a while, don't they? Maybe not today or tomorrow, but eventually life takes over.'

He couldn't argue with her observations. If it wasn't happening to an individual, Dean was under no illusion that news faded fast.

'He saw an opportunity,' he said with dawning realisation. 'With the food crisis. And RED Co.'s distribution programme.'

'Yes.'

'My god.' Dean let the words hang. They seemed poignant, not only for the divinity of their surroundings, but the scale of what was going on beyond its walls.

After a long moment Dean spoke again. He knew the here and now, the past—their past—was still a mystery he needed to uncover.

'So what happened after the town? Did you see your father again?'

'We both did,' Susan said as she tried to brush dust from her dress. 'We were taken back to his laboratory. That day a frightened little girl was reunited with her father. And a nosy journalist had a brain wipe.'

'Great.'

Contempt fell from him but there was plenty more in the Oast House. His throat tasted acrid, his mind a swirling vortex of barely contained anger. He had become product, his brain adjusted to serve the needs of those at RED Co. They'd blasted the town and removed Green's mistake. He was the fly in the ointment, the maggot in meat. His stomach felt bitter and hollow.

Fuck, he needed a drink.

Susan, it seemed, wanted to air thoughts that had been locked away for a while.

'It's hard to believe it,' she murmured. 'My father's creation is loose in the world.'

'Only because he opened its cage,' Dean said.

'Sample Ten?' Susan surmised.

'Yes,' Dean replied.

'It makes sense to me,' Susan said.

'How so?'

'I have spent many years with my father, in his labs, little more than a rat that he professes to love.' The tears were back and this time she removed her shades, her fingers pressing into her sockets in an attempt to stem the tide. The pause that followed was stretched out, her fight to regain composure internalised. Then she looked up at the ceiling and her chest shuddered as control returned. 'He loves me. I know that. In his own way all of this is born out of that love. But somewhere along the line it went bad. Passion and grief became obsession and it's poisoned the man I once knew.'

'Sample Ten was his attempt to save the world, Susan,' he said. 'Seems he's managed to destroy it instead.'

Susan's sobs reverberated about the church, made only less heartbreaking by the cries and growls outside the walls.

* * *

When Susan had cried herself out, Dean gently probed her for information on what had happened to her after his brain had been scrubbed clean.

She told him a harrowing tale that involved years of ritualistic monitoring and conditioning. Her father, it seemed, had gone mad by this point, a suggestion given credence by his reluctance to let go of his theories of introducing Sample 10 into the food chain in order to study its effects.

'It was all done in the name of love.' Her voice almost made the statement convincing. But it was unstable, the foundations in danger of rotting away and bringing the whole pretence down to earth.

'Love comes in many guises, Susan,' Dean said. 'People kill in its name, your father among them.'

'Yes,' she said but the word was clipped, as though warning him as to how fragile her tolerances were at that moment. 'I ran away once it became clear. It wasn't an easy thing to do after years confined in a lab and its grounds. My friends all wore white suits and biochem masks. Nothing was as it seemed.'

'You were brave to run,' he conceded.

'Don't patronise me!' Her voice was sudden and bright in the dull, oppressive surroundings. Dean held up a hand to calm her. The last thing he wanted was for those things in the street to find religion and come to church.

'Okay,' he said. 'Take it easy. I'm sorry. I'm still learning to walk through all of this shit too.'

She appeared to deflate, as though his words had punctured her mounting anger. Her hands gripped the bevelled edge of the pew in front of her; the slim pale fingers were stark against the dark wood.

'Yes,' she said, nodding. 'Yes, you're right. I'm sorry.'

'Don't apologise, Susan,' he said softly. 'I merely meant that it must've been hard for you to leave. In some ways that place had become your home.'

'It was a prison.' This time there was no malice, it was a statement, testament to her experience.

'How did you escape?'

'I don't know,' she said. The confusion in her face helped reinforce the response. 'It's a crazy blur. How I got to the city is even more vague.'

'It's a miracle you survived the journey,' Dean said.

'There are no miracles,' she said. 'Only the deeds of bad men.'

'Like your father?'

'Yes.'

'Yet he is the only person who can stop all of this,' Dean said. 'You know that, right?'

'What are you saying?'

'Can you find your way back to the base?' Dean asked.

'Why would I want to do that?'

'The answers are there,' he said. 'Not in here. Not out on the streets. He'll have papers or notes, information that may help us to stop this mess. Maybe even reverse it.

'I don't know if I can go back,' she said weakly. 'I don't know how I got out of there. Did I escape or has something worse happened there? Something that made it easier for me to get free?'

Well, if the truth be known, I'm counting on the latter of those scenarios. I'm hoping the place—your father—got a taste of its own enzyme, dear girl.

'Then tell me where it is,' Dean suggested instead. 'And I'll go.'

'I can't remember.'

Dean tried to keep his temper caged, and sucked in a breath. He did it.

Just.

'Look, Susan,' he said keeping his voice as neutral as possible. 'The food is contaminated. Having a meal is going to become a game of Russian roulette. Soon we'll either starve or be eaten. The options are off the shit-scale, you get me?'

She didn't reply.

'So,' he pressed, 'you remember anything? A landmark? A road name?'

'I recall a castle on the horizon,' she said after a moment.

'Which direction?'

Her brow furrowed in concentration. 'South-west.'

'Lots of castles in the UK,' he pointed out. 'Can you describe it?'

She closed her eyes to help recollection. 'Neat and well kept. It looked lived in.'

'A round keep in the middle?' Dean asked as an image came to mind.

'You know it?' Susan's face showed fear and relief but didn't settle on either.

'Yes,' he said. 'Windsor Castle. Thirty miles on the M4. Fifty minutes' drive on a good day.'

Good and bad days have been recently redefined, Deano. It's more a case of being able to see a day through without ending up mutated or dead.

He bypassed Jenna and forced himself to focus on hope. But it was a tough gig.

'I have another question,' he said.

'What?'

'You staying on your own or coming with me?'

Outside the fusion of ebbing cries and the wail of car alarms came to them, the hideous din barely filtered by beautiful stained glass.

'Guess,' she said with an uneasy smile.

BACK TO NOWHERE

Dean hot-wired an old VW Polo they found parked behind the church. To move without being seen, they'd used an exit that was situated just to the left of the altar where a small office lay in disarray. No sign remained of its occupants. Dean made a guess at what had happened to them.

The VW fired after the engine gave out a few hitches.

Susan sat beside him and stared ahead, her thoughts as much a mystery as the events of the past few hours. Something else stirred inside Dean as he put the car into reverse and manoeuvred into position, ready to leave the church grounds. He couldn't quite place the sensation; it was evasive, not wanting to land.

It involved Susan's account of her life before it collided with his. He had an affinity with her he couldn't explain, that just did not make sense.

She had gaps in her story; he had gaps in his life. They made quite a pair. Yet, at that moment, he made a decision not to delve too deeply. They had an uncertain journey ahead.

If they could navigate their way out of the city, the M4 would take them south-west, crossing into Royal Berkshire. There Windsor castle, home to English royalty since the 11th century, would be their guide to less resplendent locations, Green's clandestine base of operations.

There was no denying that their path was treacherous and fraught with risk, but he smoothed his nerves by telling himself that a young woman had made the journey to the city without issue.

'Fortune favours the brave', he recalled someone saying once. He only hoped fortune held some favour in reserve for the foolhardy.

* * *

The roads were a confused network of bent metal and shredded flesh. The VW was faced with a maze of spent vehicles, many of which were parked up. Dean began to think that maybe Susan had become a boon, chasing away the curse of the past few hours.

That the VW was able to navigate a route through thinned traffic made clear to Dean that the onset of the crisis had happened well before rush hour. He shivered when he thought of how they'd be able to escape had this all kicked off at noon. They'd be trapped like mice in the paws of a spiteful cat, waiting for the jaws to close upon them.

There was no escaping the hideous images beyond the windscreen. Wads of meat lay strewn about the streets, or slapped to walls and traffic signs. Discarded limbs jutted from hedges or doorways. Dean noted in disgust that he wasn't the only one whose fortune had appeared to change. Everywhere murders of crows pecked at the pale meat; some didn't even acknowledge the vehicle as it passed.

The balance had shifted, that much was clear. Mankind wasn't on thin ice; he was below the surface, hands scrabbling at the frozen barrier between life and death.

Susan remained quiet and thoughtful throughout the exodus from the city. She finally broke her silence, startling Dean in the process.

'How far is Windsor?' Susan asked.

'Twenty nine miles, give or take,' he said. 'How the hell did you get here? On foot?'

'I don't know,' she said. 'I wish I did. I hate mysteries.'

'I'm partial to an Agatha Christie or two.' He made an attempt to smile. It seemed wrong when people about them lay torn to pieces.

'Life is mystery enough for any man,' she said. 'My father used to say that. It was his doctrine as he pursued his work.'

'He sought to unlock doors to bad rooms,' Dean said.

'In the end, maybe,' she conceded. 'Love and obsession are siblings when there is no reason or restraint. My father sought to cure me of disease. But it wasn't enough. He made it his duty to rid the world of Progeria.'

'He saw it as an enemy,' Dean said carefully. 'The thing that wanted to take away the person he loved more than anything.'

'It's gone beyond science,' she said, chewing her lip. 'It became personal.'

And now others are paying the price. Contaminated food was being distributed under the guise of alms and ruining people, creating monsters bent only on brutality and destruction. The monsters created as a consequence were as much Green's children as the woman sat next to him, out-of-control offspring that stood as a terrible testament to the professor's final descent into madness.

'You notice something?' Susan pulled him from his reverie.

'Hard not to,' he said grimly.

'I don't mean the bodies,' Susan said softly.

'What?'

'No creatures,' she said.

Dean stopped the car and stared ahead. For as far as he could see the street leading out of the city was devoid of movement. It was an eerie sight, one that would've been better suited to a Richard Matheson novel, but no matter how many times he scanned the scene, he found no sign of the creatures.

'What does it mean?' Susan asked. The tone of her voice led Dean to believe this was mere rhetoric.

He answered regardless.

'It means we're clear to leave,' he said, slipping the car into first gear.

They began moving again.

* * *

The extent of the chaos came as they reached the city outskirts. As tower blocks became suburbs, the terraced houses displayed similar scenes of carnage. Front doors were open, windows smashed, and contents of buildings and people littered the street.

'Holy shit,' Dean muttered. 'This hasn't stayed in the city. It's fucking everywhere.'

'Let's just keep moving,' Susan said as she looked at the hopeless vista. Tears were in her eyes and, as they bubbled over her golden irises, Dean was reminded of watching a sun shower in spring. It brought with it an aching sense of grief, as though her mourning for the world that was had already begun. He reached across and put his hand on hers. She didn't move it away.

'Look,' he said, 'your father started this and I'm convinced that, somewhere, he'll have the means to stop it. All we have to do is find it.'

'I'm not sure I can go back into that place,' she muttered.

'I'm not asking you to,' he said. 'Just find it for me and I'll go and see what I can do.'

It sounded simpler than it really was and commanded brashness he really didn't think he possessed. But it was time to step up to the plate, find some way to stop all of this before the authorities lost control, and help was no longer able to swoop from the sky with the scream of jet engines and the staccato roar of a chain gun.

'Okay.' She seemed to relax a little and he moved his hand away, though part of him didn't want to. Part of him needed the contact of another person. For some time he'd only ever craved the company of Ol' Jim. But, like everyone about him, times were changing.

As usual, thoughts of his companion of so many years had him yearning. Soon it would be a physical thing, a thing of tremors and sweats and muscle cramps.

He paid careful attention to the stores he passed for the next few miles. Heart scudding, he eventually found a Tesco Express, its window now diamonds on the pavement outside. He pulled the car over to the side of the road and told Susan to lock the doors.

'Where are you going?' Panic lay in those golden eyes. He spoke softly to placate her.

'We need some provisions,' he explained. 'We don't know what the hell is happening out there. We need to eat and this place will have dried goods with a long shelf life. Stuff that isn't likely to be contaminated.'

'Why can't I come with you?'

'Because I don't want to be responsible for anything happening to you,' he said.

Christ, he carried enough guilt around with him. He didn't want to add another bag to the saddle.

'I can look after myself.' Her tone was defiant, hurt.

'I wouldn't doubt that for a second,' Dean said. 'I just need to be sure you're kept safe. You know where the base is, right? I can't find it without you. I can't stop this without you.'

This placated her to some degree but he could see she was far from happy. She crossed her arms and turned away from him. As he walked away from the car and to the store, he heard the car door locks thud shut.

Satisfied, he stepped inside.

* * *

Inside the store, chaos reigned supreme. At first Dean thought he was too late and the shop had been subject to looting and vandalism.

Then he saw the blood. And the remains lying amid the produce scattered in the aisles. The power was still on and the insect buzz from the freezers cut the air. The lighting made the scene blatant and the gore more vivid. There were three bodies in total, their sex indistinguishable, skin and clothing reduced to ribbons.

Dean went to the checkout. The staff access door was coded so he climbed over the counter, kicking over a display case. Lottery scratch cards fluttered onto the tiles. Dean picked one up and looked at it, his face pensive. Scratch cards were a thing of the past, of that he was sure. From this point on luck was determined not by scratching off silver panels on a lurid yellow promise, but whether you ran into a creature hell bent on getting to know your innards.

Perversely he still scratched away the silver windows and shook his head in disbelief as they revealed he'd won a hundred pounds. Another day it would have been a victory but now it was irony screwed up tight and rammed down this throat.

Dean tossed the card with the others, his smile grim and his eyes vague for a few moments as he sought some time to adjust to the enormity of what was happening. He purged his sense of loss with a drawn-out sigh and stood. He went to the shelf where spirits were kept. Sure enough, Ol' Jim was there with several brethren. Dean retrieved a bottle, unscrewed the cap and sank half of it.

His words of platitude to keep Susan in the car were true up to a point. Yes, he needed her safe in order to ensure he found the base. And yes, he didn't want to feel responsible if anything should happen to her. But it was his need to get reacquainted with Ol' Jim—to ensure the reunion had a degree of intimacy—that really fed his enthusiasm for her to stay in the car. It was bad enough the populace were eating each other, let alone that she put faith in a stranger who was some fucking alcoholic looking for his next bender.

No, better this way, for both of them. He lined the bottles on the counter and left via the staff door, walking round to the front of the store and putting the bottles into two carrier bags that he'd grabbed en route. He kept the opened bottle with him. His body was enjoying the warmth Ol' Jim provided. And, the way he saw it, being over the limit wasn't exactly going to be a priority for local law enforcement these days.

Leaving the bags by the front entrance, he then claimed a basket and went farther into the store checking the packages. He found dehydrated soups, dried pasta, packets of rice, anything that had a significant sell-by date. This meant it had been in storage for some time, and before Green had used RED Co. to sow his heinous seed. Or that was Dean's theory, anyway.

It was a surreal event—Dean wandering through the devastated shop, basket laden with goods in one hand, bottle of Ol' Jim in the other. A sign of the times, he mused as he gathered the last of the supplies, bagged them and left the shop.

But not before leaving thirty pounds on the counter. The gesture was a token but it made him feel better.

He'd leave the rest of his comfort to Ol' Jim.

* * *

Their trip on the motorway was a surreal event that consisted of driving at great speeds only to be slowed down by vehicles abandoned in a variety of lanes or on the hard shoulder. In some cases, the vehicles, cars and trucks were charred shells, their occupants black and wizened mummies contorted in agony on the asphalt. At this, Susan would turn away and whimper in despair. Dean was relieved to see the signs that would take him off of the motorway. Somehow the thought of being trapped on the endless stretch of road unnerved him. This was as much a highway to hell as it was an escape from it. On a few occasions the vast road was subject to a huge pile-up, the wreckage reminiscent of a traffic jam that had been subject to a carpet bombing. During these times, Dean steered a careful route through the devastated remnants of vehicles and people. On occasions, where petrol had splashed out across the highway and gave off a wavering fume, this was a perilous task.

Dean exited the M4 at Slough and they made their way through the Berkshire countryside, following brown tourist signs for Windsor Castle. About them, the city was a thing of the past and fields and broad oak trees sculpted the landscape into a thing of great beauty. Had Dean not been through the hell of the past twenty-four hours, it would have been difficult to think that anything could possibly be wrong.

Rising from the rural landscape, Windsor Castle stood bold and as impervious to time as the landscape around it. The exterior bailey wall, one of three, masked the circular keep Dean knew to be at its heart. The sun played on the surface of walls hewn from Bagshot Heath stone, turning the castle to auburn, and despite the circumstances, Dean relished the spectacular intrusion.

'There is the castle,' Dean said as though his passenger couldn't see the splendour shimmering through the windscreen. 'How far is it from here?'

He slowed the car to give her time to think.

'I'm really not sure,' she said. 'If we keep heading south-east I'm hoping I'll get some landmarks.'

'Okay,' he said nudging the car onwards. They drove past the towers, the road taking them east for a few miles and putting the castle to their left.

'You enjoy your whiskey, don't you?' Susan said. 'How long have you been drinking?'

The questions were so unexpected, so conversational, he answered without hesitation.

'As long as I can remember.' He paused then as realisation hit him. He kept his eyes ahead as guilt tickled his belly. 'How did you know?'

'Booze breath,' she said. 'My father likes his whiskey too. Perhaps it was the only thing that kept him going for as long as he has.'

'I got some from the shop,' Dean said, feeling his neck flush like a school kid caught stealing sweets from the counter.

'That figures,' she said with a small smile. 'We all have our vices. Or so I'm told.'

Resignation infused her voice, and Dean recognised a sense of loss in her so deep, so profound, that his heart felt even heavier than usual. This was not a woman; it was a child in a woman's body, a human being who had spent most of her life in a laboratory, deprived of the experiences that all would take for granted.

'Is there anyone special?' It was clumsy but he didn't know how else to put it.

'No.'

It was simple, inoffensive, as though such a thing had never before crossed her mind. Yet her breathing appeared rapid, indicating that she may have been thinking it now.

'There was nothing like that in the lab,' she whispered. 'Just tests, always the tests, and the fitness regimes.'

'Relationships aren't all they're cracked up to be,' Dean said to try ease her discomfort.

'Would be nice to come to that decision myself,' she said. 'Would be nice to live more than just a contrived life.'

Dean remained focused on the road ahead, the trees and hedgerows masking much of the surrounding countryside. He listened to her quietly weeping beside him, wondering if it would be right to offer her some comfort, the hand in the lap for example, or if such a thing would just make things worse for her. There was a fine line between comfort and pity, after all.

'Pull over,' she said.

'Have you seen something you recog—'

'Just pull over, dammit!'

Her cry had him slamming on the brakes and the squeal of tyres was high and long, the bonnet dipping and making the horizon sink for a few moments. No sooner had the car stopped than Susan was pushing open the door and staggering away.

Dean jumped from the vehicle and went after her. He almost caught up with her as she climbed over a wide fence that yielded to a cornfield. She was too quick. He clambered clumsily over the gate, Susan's sobs mixed in with the hiss of corn stalks stirred by the breeze.

'Susan!' he called as she disappeared into the thick crops. 'Wait up! Whatever I said, I'm sorry!'

Dean followed her path, husks and stems swept aside and crushed at her passing. He saw her up ahead, arms flailing away at the corn, her movement erratic. He increased his speed and caught up with her, grabbing her slight shoulder and turning her body to face him in one fluid movement.

She knocked his hands away and slapped him across his face; her eyes moist. Grief and exertion flushed her cheeks.

'What the hell's the matter with you?' he said, rubbing at his face.

'I never wanted this!' she yelled. 'I'm cursed. My life is a sham, an experiment. I'm not a person, I'm product!'

'That's not true,' he said.

'You don't believe that.' She sobbed. 'How can you? You don't know me.'

'That doesn't mean I can't get to know you, Susan,' he said, stepping closer. She didn't move away. 'Things are different, look at what is happening. We have to stick together. It may seem bad, but you and me, we're all there is at the moment. You came looking and you found me. That has to mean something, right?'

Her body sagged, and she fell into him. He held her, her body slight and firm against his frame. As he stroked her hair, pieces of masonry and corn husk tickled his palm.

'It's not that bad an idea,' she said into his shoulder. 'Having you around.'

She pulled away slightly and lifted her face to his, and he saw the way her lips parted. He bent his head down and kissed her gently, brushing her lips with his tongue. She kissed back, the movement insistent and clumsy, giving an indication of her inexperience.

Dean slipped the straps of the summer dress over her pale shoulders and gravity did the rest. She wore no bra, and the nipples of her small breasts were pink and erect, her skin, alabaster.

His hands found her buttocks, cupped them, kneaded them, and she adjusted her stance allowing his thigh to slip between her legs, where she began to rub her sex against him, small sharp moans coming from the back of her throat.

Dean's loins stirred, responding to Susan's movements and her moans of pleasure. They both fell to their knees, Dean pulling her white cotton thong down over her thighs before tracing his hands over skin, silky to the touch. His fingers moved between her legs where her vagina was wet and allowed his probing digits to slip over her clitoris and his mouth suckled her right breast. She yelped with delight, her hips gyrating, and her sex slathering against his fingers.

Susan's head fell onto his shoulder, her hands pulling open his jeans. Dean moved his hands away from her and helped her remove the irritating denim and underwear. He lay on his back, his penis pointing skyward, her vagina hovering over it as she sought to straddle him. She placed her hands on his chest and began to tentatively ease him into her. Her golden eyes were wide, her mouth forming a quivering O as she brought her thighs down onto his hips. He pushed up to meet her and she cried out in both pain and pleasure. She was tight and hot about him and his penis relished every squeezing second, his hands sought her buttocks again, forcing her forwards as he came to meet her, his length stroking against her clitoris, the right angle, the right moment, she came fast, the sensation too exquisite, too delicious to fight. Her short, sharp shriek was overridden by more moans as Dean continued to push against her, pressing the small of her back until he exploded inside her with a shuddering groan.

He lay, shivering, with Susan pressed against him, his organ still inside her. He stroked her back, feeling her skin goose under his touch.

'You okay?' he asked tentatively.

'Yes,' she said into his neck. 'That was nice.'

She tightened her grip on him and he began to harden again.

'Can we do it again?' she asked.

'Oh, absolutely,' he said.

* * *

The VW was moving again, the road noise filling the silence inside. It wasn't a difficult silence, the kind between two people who had perhaps made a mistake and were now sitting in a state of remorse. It was a contented, sated silence, where each moment slid past and added to the memories, the rightness, of it all.

They had sex three times; the last was one of exploration, where he had not penetrated her but kissed and caressed her to a final climax. He felt he owed her in some way, for the deeds of her father, the deeds of man, somehow showing her that life wasn't about cells and surgical tables, it was about love and the warmth of two people.

In those moments, Dean found something else, grounding, tantamount to an epiphany. He wasn't sure if this was due to world's end or the mere presence of the beautiful young woman who had kindled a new kind of hope in him.

'The base is up ahead,' Susan said.

'You remember?' Dean replied. The road appeared to stretch out for some distance and there were no signs indicating any points of reference.

'Yes,' she said. 'There is a right turn after a few hundred yards.'

'Okay,' he said, leaning forward so he could anticipate the turn-off. 'What made you recall it?'

'I don't know,' she admitted. 'But it's there, all of it.'

'One more thing to add to the memories,' he said, turning to her briefly.

'This isn't as good as the last,' she said with a tiny smile.

'Maybe not,' he said. 'But it may help stop what's happening. And that can't be a bad thing, right?'

'Yes,' she said. 'Here we are.'

The turn-off came from nowhere and Dean had to apply the brakes firmly so the car didn't overshoot. There was a long innocuous path, nothing more than a dirt track, snaking uphill until it went right and disappeared between two knolls.

Dean drove the car up the trail, the tyres churning yellow-brown dust in their wake. As they neared the summit, Susan placed her hand on his thigh.

She's scared. She's returning to a place that is both home and prison. And she wants it to be neither from this point on.

He put his hand on hers and gently squeezed.

'It'll be okay, Susan,' he said softly. 'You'll see.'

'I do.'

This made him smile with a sincerity he had not experienced in what felt like a lifetime.

* * *

They came to the gates after five minutes of sending dust across the landscape. The huge mesh frames were open and interior of the compound appeared still. Realisation that the reason Susan had been able to escape because everything here had gone to shit comforted him. Sure, they might get eaten, but they wouldn't end up prisoners. Dean wondered when such odds had become a favourable premise. He chose to move on.

'Stay in the car,' Dean said. 'I'll go and check it out.'

'I'll come with you,' she said. 'I don't want to be alone.'

Dean didn't argue. He wanted Susan with him, he couldn't explain the powerful bond they seemed to share, and they had become inseparable. Susan seemed to be the new drug of choice, the pending apocalypse: the new matchmaker. Dean felt like a love struck teenager, his thoughts consumed, intoxicated, by Susan. None of it made sense; it was as though he always known her, a soul mate in the truest sense.

They eased from the car, leaving the doors wide. With trepidation they moved together, Susan coming to meet him at the bonnet and taking hold of his hand. Her action got his heart pumping faster than the fear.

Trucks were parked beyond the gate and debris lay scattered about the asphalt. Buildings, low and long, created a dull grey border, and a few of them had been gutted by fire. The whole atmosphere was one of abandonment and desolation.

A few bodies were visible. Some were torn open but others added mystery as well as dread. Dean went to one of them, caution making his steps tentative. It was sitting on the tarmac, its back slumped against the wall of one of the buildings, as though taking a rest after the slaughter.

Dean knelt beside the figure and looked it over. At some point the person it once was wore a lab coat, but the body wasn't unrecognisable due to mutilation, instead it was difficult to fathom because transformation had contorted its face into a burlesque parody of a human being.

Its eyes were black and wide, the final stages of metamorphosis, and the jaw had jutted forward enough for it to dislocate. Dean was fascinated by the colour of the creature's skin. It appeared as ash. He looked about him and found a discarded biro, and used it to probe the creature's face. Where the pen made contact, the skin disintegrated, the grey powder drifting like smoke in the air.

'Why is it dead?' he asked Susan. 'Was this happening when you left here?'

'I can't remember,' she said with a shudder. 'It might be the only reason I got out alive.'

Dean stood. The entrance to the main base, a beige door marked laboratory in large, bold lettering, was visible only a few hundred metres away.

'Will you be guide?' he asked Susan. She nodded.

'Then lead the way,' he said softly. 'I'm with you.'

'Good,' she said with a small smile and retook his hand, squeezing it for comfort. Then, they made their way to the main building.

* * *

The scenes in the compound did little to prepare them for the devastation inside the main building. The wide corridor was an elongated charnel house. The floor had originally been a clinical white, but now black blood was splurged as far as he could see. Then he saw the bones, gnawed clean by many teeth.

'My God,' he said.

'God had no hand in this,' Susan said. 'Come on. The lab is this way.'

She moved forward, her sense of urgency evident in the way she pulled him along. Doorways passed by, and each time he risked peering inside one of the rooms, Dean was met with the same—skeletal remains littering the spaces like the cave of a fairy tale ogre.

There were not just bones, of course. The ashen shapes were here as well, clothing dark with black blood and bodies petrified where their demise, in whatever guise it had come, had left them.

Dean's mind churned; it had a lot to digest. Under normal circumstances Ol' Jim would come knocking but, for the first time in an age, Dean had no inclination to draw back the dead bolt. Not yet at least.

'So where are we likely to find information?' he asked.

'Father kept his more valuable records locked away in his office,' Susan explained without looking back at him. He watched the way her dress swayed in time with her buttocks, and his mind drifted to moments, not so long ago, when he had his hands all over them as she rode him like a pony.

Not now, Deano! For fuck's sake!

He blocked out the thought but promised himself that they would pay the cornfield another visit once they'd found Green's papers. After that he didn't have much of a plan.

Maybe you'd better get one, Deano. Sure, banging the virgin daughter of a deranged scientist might be a decent start to the end of the world, but how about finding a way to stop it from happening first?

Jenna was always the killjoy. Yet there was no doubt they would have to move fast once Susan had located the information to arrest the effects of Green's experiments. Somehow they had to find someone in authority, someone who could decipher Green's work and reverse what had been done.

He dipped into his pocket and checked his phone again.

Still dead. Like most of the fucking population, right?

'Is there a communications room, Susan?'

'Yes,' she said. 'It's in the north corridor not far from my father's office.'

'Then we should go there,' he said. 'Once we get what we need.'

'Okay.'

He sensed necessity in her now. The hand pulling him along slipped from his as, at the far end of the corridor, a door with the words Professor Green stencilled onto a pane of frosted glass came into view.

'Susan, wait!' Dean hissed as she moved towards the door at great pace. She'd become too focused on her goal, to find a means for righting all of her father's ills. Their excursion may only have brought them bones and ash so far but it was far from being designated safe.

A fact that became all too clear only ten seconds later.

* * *

The creature lumbered from one of the side rooms. The thing was large, more than six-five, and its bulk filled the door frame. Remnants of clothing - tattered beige trousers with gold and white piping, and a shirt to match - flapped about the creature's shape. The shirt was hanging open, the bulbous, undulating gut beneath having forced open all of the buttons. The weight of a gold security shield dragged the material to one side, exposing the putrid flesh beneath.

Dean reached out for Susan and snaked an arm about her slim waist. He yanked her backwards and she gave out a short sharp squeal of surprise as they both landed on the floor. Despite the menace it exuded, the creature appeared disorientated and fragile, a fact that became all too apparent as it tripped and fell into the opposite wall and, incredibly, exploded as it met the concrete, the uniform material hanging in the air like a ghost as a great, billowing cloud of ash swept through the hallway.

It passed over Dean and Susan, settling on them like silt on a flood plain. Dean's instinct was to frenetically paw at it, to get rid of this awful debris lest he be contaminated too.

They stood and Susan joined him as he dusted himself down, but it was a token gesture. There was just too much of it.

Dean spotted a water fountain a few yards away, a silver basin with a chrome faucet. Ignoring the blood splatters on the stainless steel, he rinsed his face, neck and hair. He beckoned Susan to him, and helped her do the same.

'This doesn't make sense,' he said. 'What's happening here?'

'They're starving,' she said bluntly. 'They have nothing to sustain them.'

Dean rubbed his brow. Of course! The evidence was there all along; the bones had been picked clean, no scrap of flesh left behind. In some way it gave him hope. If those who survived this mess could get clear of the towns and cities, these creatures would simply cease to exist. The balance would be restored as nature intended.

'Then it's a waiting game,' he said. 'They'll die out.'

'Solves nothing in the short term,' she reminded him. 'Nor does it stop it all happening again.'

'Find your father's work?'

'You got it,' she said with a tired smile.

'Susan?' he said carefully.

'I know,' she said.

'What?' he asked, unable to hide his surprise.

'That my father may be dead,' she clarified.

'It's a very real possibility,' he agreed.

'The man who was my father died long ago,' she said with resignation. 'Perhaps it is a blessing.'

She ran her fingers through her damp hair and Dean watched her, admiring her strength. God, she was beautiful. The sight of her consumed him; the small swell of her breasts, her milky thighs. Dean wanted to just step up to her and relieve her of the dress and take her, hard and wanton, until he was spent.

'We need to move,' she said, turning back to her father's office. It killed the moment, leaving Dean looking after her as she walked away, his breathing heavy and his face flushed.

Shit! What's happening to me? His mind was trying to keep up with the staccato rhythm in his chest. Since the cornfield, since his time with Susan—in Susan—he was like a child again, his thoughts mesmerised by her presence and his need to be with her once more.

Am I in love? Is this what it really feels like?

Let's get this right, Deano, Jenna said, *the world is dying and you wanna go and play hide the hose with your newfound girlfriend? Man up! Get a fucking grip!*

It wasn't Jenna who finally got him moving, it was Susan.

Her scream caught him unawares and his heart froze. Ahead she had stepped into her father's office, and was standing just beyond the threshold. The door opened inwards and she stood side on, peering right, as her hands came up to her face.

Dean moved, his shoes slipping on the linoleum and giving out small rodent squeaks. He got to Susan and put his arms about her, protecting her from the terrible thing she had discovered.

The desk was neat and tidy, papers arranged in piles—pens and pencils lined with their points facing the door. It was a scene of scientific serenity, organisation and conformity in one.

But all of this was shattered by the severed head sitting in the middle of the table.

* * *

The head belonged to Professor Green. It had been nailed to the table by a letter opener, the handle of which jutted out of his bald and bloodied crown, and the blade was a vertical slat of silver visible through the professor's open mouth. Dean was fascinated by the macabre sight. Unable to pull his gaze away, he could not believe the brutality of it, even after everything he'd witnessed. Green's eyes were rolled upwards as though, even in death, the maverick professor was searching his mind for answers.

Green's body was still sitting in the chair behind its desk, hands gripping the arms, knuckles white and fat. His wrists had been cruelly bound to the arm rests. Copper wire cut deep into the pale skin, leaving red welts that appeared livid even post mortem. The professor's neck was a ragged stump, the edged chewed and twisted, and Dean quickly realised the head had been torn from his body.

Susan shuddered against Dean's chest, her shoulders moving up and down as a guttural sound emerged from lips that were pressed into his breast pocket, her breath heating his skin beneath, making his nipple erect. He didn't know what to say, didn't know what words of comfort would possibly fit such an event. He had a go but his attempt to appease sounded hollow and useless.

'Easy, Susan,' he said. 'It'll be okay, baby. You'll see.'

Pathetic, Deano, truly pathetic! But it's okay. I love you. I always have. I always will.

Dean froze. The voice in his head was spiteful and harsh. But it was not his mocking irritant of a sister.

It belonged to Susan.

His mind buckled, a dizzying, brain-tearing sensation that had both of his hands clamping down on his skull as his cry of agony pierced the air. His knees hit the floor, one of them popping on impact, but the world had become smoke and, for a while, he drifted away with it.

* * *

About him there are shadows. They dance like motes against bright sunlight, confusing and dumbfounding.

Then voices join them, a thick cacophony that only adds to the disorientation, making it difficult to find any sense of time or place. But no sooner do they come, the voices thin out, dissipating like a hoar frost at the touch of a spring sun. One voice takes precedence; it is whispered and insistent, coated with layers of pleasure and malice. A hushed voice.

Susan's voice.

'Oh, my,' she breathes, 'how could I have waited so long, for this, for you?'

Dean is aware, yet it is not corporeal, it is an awareness of the mind. Susan is close to him, inside his head, yet he knows that elsewhere he is inside her, a physical act of coitus of her choosing.

'What's happening?' He struggles to understand why; far away, he feels great pleasure and searing agony. He leaves trying to explore such nuances for the moment and concentrates only on Susan's dialogue. It fascinates and paralyses, making him a prisoner.

'What's happening is what is meant to be,' she says coyly. 'We are one, joined and inseparable. You should not be surprised. It has been this way for some time.'

'I don't—'

'Understand? Yes, I know,' she says, 'but you will understand, Dean. You will understand because I will show you.'

She pauses for a second and his mind is filled with a drawn-out moan. Again, in that far off place, he feels a spectacular sensation, and he hears his own voice join in with Susan's delight.

'Now, where were we?' she asks. 'Oh, yes, the matter of our being together. I was going to show you things. Seems only fair as you've given me so much of yourself in such a short space of time.'

The pleasure is back in her voice, and he can feel his own resurface. Whatever is happening in the world from which he is currently divorced it appears to be in a constant state of flux.

'I never knew you before today,' he protests. 'I knew of you, sure, but I don't remember ever meeting you.'

'But I told you we'd met,' she says. 'Are you saying you don't believe me? Are you calling me a liar?'

He senses her petulance; it seems the child in her finds his words dismissive and hurtful.

'No,' he says hastily. 'I'm confused. I have gaps.'

'Of course.' She is calm again; the storm has been quelled in moments. 'I can show you what has been forgotten.'

His vista changes with the suddenness of a thrown switch. Gone are the shadows and the dancing light. Instead he sees a young girl talking to a man in a lab coat. The girl is behind a glass screen and in the corner is a cot. The man sings to her and the tune is achingly familiar and fills him with a quiet rage.

The girl walks to the cot and curls up beneath a duvet; she appears to drift off to sleep almost immediately, her body twitching.

The vision changes, and now there is a compound. Inside it there are many trucks. Susan is there, hiding behind two fuel barrels as foodstuff is unloaded from the back of the trailers. Time has moved on. She is older, in her teens, and wears jogging pants and a T-shirt. Her body is lithe and the skin on her bare arms is slick with sweat from a long run down many corridors.

'I know this,' he says.

'Yes.'

'But these memories are mine,' he says but he does not sound sure. 'No, not memories, dreams.'

'Wrong. So wrong.'

The images waver and transform. Susan looks as she does now. She is running from the compound, the gate is receding; the base behind her pumps smoke into the sky. There is no fear evident, in fact she stops and spins on the spot, clapping her hands together with glee.

'These are not dreams,' she says to him. 'Nor are they memories. They are my message to you. My message that we have been one since we watched Gullcrest burn.'

'You mean telepathically?' Dean is dumbfounded. Despite everything, it all seems unreal, the stuff of children's books. 'How is that possible?'

'I do not know the science behind it,' she says casually. 'And I did not raise it with my father. It was my little secret. I was never to be alone again. I was a lonely child and I sought out a companion. I guided you with dreams and images, led you to me with clandestine codes to hidden laboratories. That day you found me in the cell, you looked into my eyes but I saw your mind, placed myself there. From that point on you were with me, always, unaware but still there. Two lonely souls, found.'

'But I wasn't aware of you,' Dean says.

'That does not matter,' she replies. 'You saved me, I did not forget. Even if my father made sure that you did.'

'Brain wipe?' Dean recalls.

'Yes,' Susan says. 'Father likes to keep his secrets. It protects his work.'

'But now he's dead,' Dean says carefully.

'His work lives on.'

'We came here to kill that too,' Dean reminds her.

The silence is as ominous as the chuckle that shortly follows it.

'Well I guess I may have misled you a little on that particular issue,' she says. 'Only a little, mind.'

'You don't intend to find a cure? To end the suffering of so many?'

'I do,' Susan says. 'It's just a matter of perspective. We are dying, there is no doubt about that, and I intend to stop that from happening. In fact, the process has already begun.'

'How?' Dean is confused and this is echoed in his thoughts. 'We don't have the papers.'

'We have never needed the papers, silly,' Susan scoffs. 'All we needed was you.'

The lights go on in his mind and there is a whiteout. His brain tries to find refuge but it is useless. All he can do is take the pain as it comes as a thousand glass splinters piercing his cerebral cortex. He waits for a short lifetime and, when the lights dim, and the agony recedes, his vision is replaced by the cold beauty of Susan as she peers into his face, her eyes sparkling like gold ingots.

'Welcome back, lover,' she says, and Dean realises he is naked and strapped to a table as she rides him. 'Missed me?'

She does not wait for an answer. At once she is consumed in the moment and takes him, hard and fast, ignoring his cries of pain as his dislocated knee protests at her frenetic movements.

As she climaxes, her nails bite deep into his bare shoulders, drawing blood. She stoops and licks the wounds she has made.

'Where would I be without you?' she says and he can see that she means it.

Though in what context remains unclear.

* * *

'Can you get me up, please?' Dean asked.

'Haven't you had enough, lover boy?' Susan winked as she stroked his thigh.

'You know what I mean.' He was being cautious. Things were askew and he was as vulnerable as any man could be.

'Meany,' she said with a mock pout. 'I'll release you, but first we have to agree on the best way forward.'

'I don't know what you mean,' he said.

'Now, now,' she said. 'It's not the time to start getting cute.' She climbed off of him and sat on the edge of the table.

'I have been in this lab for a long time,' she said. 'Most of my life, in fact. Daddy infected me to cure me. You know this as a fact. And he did cure the disease but he created something else. Something he chose to ignore.'

'And what was that?' Dean asked. His knee hurt so badly he was having trouble concentrating.

'Why he created new life of course,' she said. 'I ceased to be the daughter he knew some time ago. Genetics is a bitch, don'tcha know? There's no room for tinkering. There are always consequences. Life will go on, it will evolve.'

She placed a hand on Dean's arm and traced her fingers over his skin, a tender act, though her face did not show emotion. It showed only recollection.

'My father never got that. He gave me potions and God knows what to keep the bad things at bay. But they were only bad because he couldn't see the good in them. The good in me. You saw it, though, didn't you? You saw what I can be? Gentle, humble, a thing of substance? Beauty?'

'Yes,' he agreed but in truth what he now saw was the result of years in the hands of a scientific madman and habitual experimentation. Susan Hadley was a monster in human form. At the moment she was his monster but she remained one all the same.

'So what's the issue?' He said it casually but inside he was quivering; exposed and vulnerable to her whims. His left knee felt as though he'd been branded, and the pain was a pulse that, under normal circumstances, would have demanded his full attention. But these were far from normal circumstances, indeed; such a premise had not existed for some time.

'Death is the issue, dearest Dean,' she chided. 'My father's legacy to me, to my kindred.'

'Kindred?' His voice could not hide his contempt. 'You mean those things?'

Susan placed her hand on his inflamed knee. And squeezed.

He screamed hard and shrill. She took her hand away.

'Show some respect,' she said simply. 'They did not ask to exist. They are as much victims as everyone else. No one chose this.'

'I didn't either,' he said. His knee was an inferno and his discomfort was making him impervious to tact.

'No,' she admitted. 'But you did choose me, Deano.'

'Don't call me that,' he said through teeth clenched with pain.

'Jenna's pet name?' Susan grinned. The lack of colour in her eyes made the jibe seem even more cruel. 'I know how much you suffered at her hands, how alone you felt. So it was with me and my life here. This is how I was able to seek you out. We have affinity, you and I. Our trials have shaped us; made us close, made us destined to be together.'

Just fucking peachy. Susan introduced her hand to his knee again. This time her palm hovered over it, teasing him.

'Careless thoughts cost lives, Deano,' she said. 'No secrets in this relationship. Ever. Not many can lay claim to that, can they?'

Dismay washed over him. Tears came to his eyes and trickled down his cheeks where they pooled upon the cold surgical steel beneath his head.

'Oh, come on,' she said, casting her golden eyes to the ceiling. 'You can't complain. You get to fuck me whenever you want. A forty-year-old drunk gets to paw a young body like this, hell I want you to fuck me. Lots.'

'You're sick,' he said.

'And you're not wrong,' she replied. 'Daddy's work has done things. To me, to my kin. DNA is mutating at an unprecedented rate. If my family don't feed within a day, they shut down. My father's idea of shelf life. Sly little fucker, wasn't he?'

'They become like those we found?' Dean recalled the ashen husks and understood. This was about survival, all right, but not of the human race. 'But how can you stop something that is now running its course?'

'Well, we need new blood,' she said with a knowing smile. 'Or rather new DNA. Your DNA, dearest. Your sperm is going to make sure life goes on.'

'You mean—' The thought was difficult to express.

'No, I don't mean—' she replied. 'Come on, Dean. You think this can be resolved as simply as having super babies? You've been watching too much Fringe, my dear. Besides, I told you, things have been done to me. Babies will not feature in this relationship. Hope that doesn't disappoint?'

He tried not to be relieved, but he was, deeply. For a moment he thought this would earn him another pat on the knee. Susan seemed too preoccupied with the process for it to register.

'I'm more than my original parts,' she said. 'But it's not enough. I'm not enough to save my kind. So I need something more. I need an independent strand of DNA that doesn't pass on the bad stuff. The hereditary line has to be broken. That's where you come in. Literally, you could say.'

'But what about the world, Susan? All those people?'

'Where was the world when we suffered, dearest?' She said it calmly, without heat, but her eyes burned with hatred. It was a sight of terrible beauty. 'The world let a scientist experiment on his daughter. The world let a small boy be bullied and beaten by his malevolent sister. I owe it nothing. We owe it nothing. I came for you and now we are together. Nothing can change that; nothing will change it.'

'Okay.' He breathed deeply, his fear, his pain making it difficult to stay focused on the decisions that had been made in his name. He just needed to get off of this fucking table.

'You will be good if I let you go, won't you, dearest? You won't force me to do anything rash?' She was swinging her legs backwards and forwards like a child sitting on a school desk while the teacher was out of the classroom. He realised that, deep down, beneath the madness brought about by a lifetime of drugs and isolation, her misplaced childhood was always keen to spend some time in the sunlight.

Was he any different? Suppressed, abused, he was the perfect recipient for her abilities. Change had brought them together but it was her designs that had made sure they would never truly be apart. He couldn't resist her; she was going to make sure of that, and in this Dean saw a way to hide beneath the resignation of this home truth, masking his intentions at least long enough to make a bid for freedom.

'I came for you, plucked you from certain death,' she said. 'Brought you back home.'

'I agree to be with you, Susan,' he said quietly. 'Will you please untie me? I want to be with you.'

She looked at him and in her gilded irises he saw a mixture of love and hope. He understood how inexorably linked they both were, mentally, physically, but in Susan he saw that deep emotion bound her to him, the love of an obsessive. It made her vulnerable but, by the same token, extremely dangerous. In this relationship love didn't just bite, it swallowed you whole and spat out the bones.

Susan jumped from the table and padded up to him. She leaned forward and planted a kiss to his forehead, her tears hitting his face like a gentle summer rain.

'I don't believe you,' she whispered.

She clamped her hands over his mouth, pinching his nostrils, shutting out any opportunity for him to breathe. Dean bucked on the table as he fought to be free of the restraints. Susan rested her cheek on his brow and, despite her closing her eyes, tears still escaped.

'Shush, my love,' she said. 'Hush, now. It'll be over soon.'

Dean thrashed for over a minute, his damaged leg snapping in the process, and his calf slapped against the table in a series of heavy thumps. His struggles became weaker as his life left him and, through it all, Susan Hadley kept her eyes shut and quietly wept.

TOMORROW NEVER COMES

Susan had left Dean Sharp on the table but not before covering him with a sheet. Later she would return to harvest his testicles. It was a contingency Susan had long hoped would never have to happen.

But contingencies were part of scientific progress. Such was life in a lab. Later that day, in the communications room, Susan sat cross-legged on a swivel chair. She had showered, and the white bathrobe she wore was warm and comforting. Her hair was tied into pigtails and in her lap was a huge bowl of popcorn.

The lights in the room were dimmed and her attentive, attractive face was lit by the bank of TV screens. As she ate popcorn Susan tried not to think too much about being alone. Thinking about such things made her feel empty and lost. It fed the insecurities of her misplaced childhood that her connection with Dean Sharp had kept at bay for so long.

Time for a new perspective. It was time for her to fill the world with beings with which she had affinity. Beings that would make sure she would never be alone again.

She giggled behind the popcorn, yet her eyes were wide with madness. The TV screens were all showing similar images, relayed from RED Co. factories all over the hemisphere.

And on each screen a series of trucks had just pulled into a compound, and eager people were unloading the foodstuff ready for distribution. Her father's creation was about to go global. He'd told her the extent of the distribution programme shortly before she'd put a letter opener through his skull. His kind of madness had sealed the fate of mankind. All that was needed was for it to be allowed to run its course.

Now, as she watched the foodstuff being whisked away to be unwittingly served up to an ignorant population, Susan continued to work her way through her snack. It would tide her over as she watched the End of Days.

Then she'd need to pay Dean a visit.

END

About the Authors

Dave Jeffery is perhaps best known for his zombie novel Necropolis Rising which has gone on to be a UK #1 Bestseller. His Young Adult work includes the critically acclaimed Beatrice Beecham Series, BBC: Headroom endorsed Finding Jericho and the 2012 Edge Hill Prize Long-listed Campfire Chillers short story collection.

Dave has contributed to several anthologies from a variety of publishers including Dark Continents Publishing, Inc., Wild Wolf Publishing, Imprint Phoenix, Hersham Horror Books, Wicked East Press, Western Legends Publishing and Hidden Thoughts Press. His work has featured alongside many zombie impresarios including John Russo (Night of the Living Dead), Tony Burgess (Pontypool) and Joe McKinney (Flesh Eaters). His short story Daddy Dearest features in the award-winning Holiday of the Dead anthology (This is Horror Awards, Best Anthology, 2012).

Necromancer: Necropolis Rising II is slated for release through Dark Continents Publishing, Inc. in October, 2013. Dave has been commissioned to produce two books and subsequent screenplays to be filmed by Silent Studios in 2014. The first of these is Contamination. His short story Ascension (featured in ALT-ZOMBIE, Hersham Horror) has been filmed by Venomous Little Man Productions, with zombies and special make up FX provided by Silent Studios, and will be released in 2013.

His website can be found at:

www.davejeffery.webs.com

His Official Face Book author page can be found at:

www.Facebook.com/DaveJefferyAuthor

Jason Wright is the CEO and Creative Director at Silent Studios and has been in the PR, promotional, photographic and production industry for over 16 years. The company is best known for their recent work on jobs like Resident Evil 6 and the Dead Island Riptide Wedding.

He is perhaps better known for his zombie craving from which Silent Studios was born and has not only wrote the story Contamination but has a few more in the wings which are due to be released over the next few years.

Contributions towards many films and projects like Rise of Jengo, The Marauders, Vicious Dead, Ascension, POV (Australia Short Film that won best film in Melbourne 2013) and many others have helped Jason and his team build their portfolio and accreditation in the horror world.

Directing films is also a strength of Jason's and at the moment amongst the projects he is involved in is ZOMBIE PLAYGROUND which is due for release in 2013.

Silent Studios and Dark Continents Publishing have joined forces to publish a new type of horror styled books and with Jason, Dave and others from both companies they will produce two books a year and subsequent screenplays to be filmed by Silent Studios.

Contamination is the first novel to be filmed and a trailer will be released in the latter part of 2013.

You can contact Jason through the Silent Studios Website

http://www.silentstudios.co.uk/

Official Face Book page Silent Studios can be found at:

www.facebook.com/silent.studios.productions

If you enjoyed this title, then you might also like:

Necropolis Rising by Dave Jeffery
ISBN 978-0977448197
Retail US$13.99, UK£8.99
It took thirty minutes for the city to die. But for the inhabitants of Birmingham City, UK the hunger will last forever. The military has sealed the city. No one is getting in. No one is getting out. But Kevin O'Connell and his team of cyber-criminals have a job to do. A job that will see them receiving a huge payout if they succeed. Or a bullet if they don't. Once inside the confines of the city O'Connell and his team are about to find out that staying alive will prove to be just as difficult as staying dead …

CPSIA information can be obtained at www.ICGtesting.com
Printed in the USA
LVOW08s0650290614

392172LV00001B/11/P